SNUFFLES:
Adventures in Atlantashedge

SNUFFLES:

Adventures in Atlantashedge

Melinda Henry

To order additional copies of this book, contact:
Xlibris Corporation
1-888-795-4274
www.Xlibris.com
Orders@Xlibris.com
91393

Contents

Chapter 1

Introduction

In the world of man and beast other worlds exist within our own realm. Hedgepeople are but one of many races coexisting within that realm. They are a race of people quiet different from what we know and think of today. Snuffles belonged to such a race of small individuals. They are strong and fearless, or so they would like you to think. Hedgepeople stand only eight inches tall, and are strong enough to move things that weighed three to four times their own size and weight. They can walk or run on two legs like human's or on two legs and two arms like a dog, which can move them along with great speed. Instead of hair they have very sharp quills of different colors that can be raised in defense. If under attack the quills protect the head and neck area from most injuries. Hedgepeople have been around since the beginning of time and are a strong and thriving race of individuals that are here to stay.

Chapter 2

Hedgelings

Can you imagine being the size of a thumbnail and blind, well that was how Snuffles was born into the world. All Hedgelings are blind and helpless at first and when born are round and formless with soft snow white quills. They cannot move on their own and they must have the constant help and care of their mother. Snuffles was just such a baby.

Snuffles slept a lot in the beginning, but soon learned that whenever he had a problem or was upset, his mother was always there to soothe and comfort him. She would feed him, clean him, play with him and keep him safe and warm. Snuffles could tell that he was not alone. Hedgelings are always born as twins or triplets, so as Snuffles lay all warm and snug with his siblings he was comforted by their closeness.

One morning when Snuffles awoke he found the world was altogether brighter. As he opened his eyes and looked around his home for the first time, he saw there were five other sets of eyes looking back at him. That was when Snuffles met his sisters and brothers for the first time. There were two the same size as Snuffles and he learned their names were Hermie and Missy, the older twins were Annabelle and Chip and then there was Mom who Snuffles knew would always be there for him, no matter what.

Mom quietly introduced each one and they quickly set about getting to know each other. As time passed by though, his family's personality became more clear. Snuffles' older sister was Annabelle. She was very bossy and was always pushing everyone around. Annabelle had cream and tan quills. Her face was light colored and she had a pointed nose, she looked exactly like mom. Snuffles' older brother was Chip, he was cinnamon in color and was twice the size of everyone else. He didn't have a lot of patience for everyone so he usually kept to himself. If your ever got into trouble though, Chip was either your best friend or your worst enemy. Hermie was Snuffles younger brother and was altogether different. He had gotten his name from Pastor Herman, the frog, who lived down the path. Pastor Herman was always croaking about one thing or the other and when Hermie was first born he always seemed to have the hiccups. This made Hermie sound as if he was croaking just like the pastor. Hermie was always ready for fun so he and Snuffles were always having a good time together. They were best of friends. The last baby born and the one Snuffles dreaded the most, was Missy. She was very spoiled and always getting into everyone's things. She would take and hide things from you and when you got them back they never seemed to be in quite the same condition as when she first took them. For instance, she took his favorite blanket, out of meanness, and when he got it back three holes now appeared in the shape of stars where there were none before. It seemed that Missy decided she wanted to look at the stars through her new tent. Girls!!!

Chapter 3

The Burrow

S nuffles home was a small, but quaint, burrow created by his mother's family in the Southern Ozarks. Most of the more affluent families lived in small villages at that time. Owning a burrow meant that your family was well off. A lot of the families that lived outside the village only had logs and caves to live in. Snuffles' home was small but their family owned it and that gave them great comfort through the seasons. The burrow had the look of an English forest cottage, it was built mainly out of stick, twigs and leaf litter. Baked mud bricks formed the foundation and the floors. This kept them high and dry in the rainy season. The floors had bamboo shafts running through them which could be heated or cooled depending on the time of year. In winter, water ran through pipes in the stove and was heated and then ran through the bamboo to warm the floor. When summer came the water ran straight from the creek and caused a cooling effect throughout the house.

The windows all had shutters to keep out bad weather and woven spider web netting to keep out insects in the summer. Mom always kept lots of flowers in her windows that helped the burrow to always seem alive.

At first, this small dark place was soft and comfortable, but as time went on and the family grew up, it was becoming very cramped. Everyone knew it would not be long before they would have to expand their dwelling. Snuffles hoped it would be his turn for a room of his own.

Each day Snuffles played throughout the house learning and exploring more of his ever expanding world. His mother loved the color green and it seemed that almost everything had the color green somewhere in it. At one end of the burrow Snuffles shared a bedroom with his younger brother Hermie. They had it fixed up really good. Their bunk beds allowed a great jumping platform, to get away from bad guys. Their dresser had a center hiding pocket that was just big enough for two little hedgelings to disappear from evil doers. The small but adequate closet was used for escaping into that dark tunnel. Snuffles and Hermie loved to pretend they were always staying one step ahead of the bad guys. To Snuffles and Hermie, their room was just about the most perfect room that any hedgeling could every ask for.

The kitchen, was probably, Snuffles most favorite place in the burrow. It was always warm and sunny and it always had the smell of something cooking. It made you happy just to be sitting inside.

There was no better cook than mom. Snuffles' favorite food was mealworms, they tasted just like candy. When mom cooked, the whole house would have such fresh aromas that you felt like you were floating on a cloud. By the time the dinner table was set everyone was dying of hunger. Annabelle was in charge of the clean-up chores at the end of each meal. Snuffles' always seemed to get stuck with sweeping and mopping the floor. He figured that it must have something to do with his dropping dishes on the floor on a regular basis. He couldn't help it. Wet dishes were really slick and whenever he would complain to Annabelle, she would just reminded him that he was lucky to get food in the first place. Sweeping and mopping the floor was a cheap price to pay for his dinner. Snuffles decided that Annabelle was probably right and with Chip standing right behind her he decided not to argue too much.

Mom shopped for food everyday and always brought home the best mealworms and June bugs that could be found. Each night she would empty her bags on the kitchen counters and everyone would pitch in to start making dinner, that is with the exception of Missy. Missy had told Snuffles that she was beyond such menial labor and that he had better get used to it. Snuffles figured that someday she'd get hers.

One day while putting away the groceries Missy had a huge tantrum. She burst into the kitchen and started to throw all the food onto the floor just because mom would not take her out for dinner that night. When mom came into the kitchen and saw the damage that Missy had caused she calmly told her that she had better start cleaning up and then turned around and left the room. Later that night when she came back in and found that Missy hadn't even started to do what she was told she got into such trouble. Chip stepped in to help enforce Mom's punishment. She had to pick up everything on the floor, make her own dinner and clean the kitchen all before she could go to bed that night. Mom then took everyone out to dinner with the exception of Missy. We could hear her screaming at the top of her lungs, "You don't love me! You're really unfair!"

Mom slowly turned around and looked at Missy and in a calm but firm voice she said, "It's because I love you that I am punishing you. You need to learn that the world does not spin around your desires. Now be a good girl and take care of the things I told you to do." As we watched, Missy's face went blank, she looked as if all the air had been let out of her balloon. She then turned around and went back inside without saying another word.

Chapter 4

The Ozark Forest

Each day Snuffles would follow his mother to the door of their burrow and watch as she shuffled off to town to get the day's food. His imagination would create wonderful images of what the town might be like. As he would watch her disappear down the path towards town he wondered what interesting and unique things were there. The stories he had heard from Annabelle and Chip about the great restaurants and stores that sold everything from June bug candy to Fire Fly Soup made his mouth water just thinking about it.

As time went on Snuffles became very curious about the outside world. So one bright, sunny morning his mother turned around and looked straight at him and said, "I think that it's time to come out into the world Snuffles. Why don't you come with me into town today. I think you're old enough now to enjoy the trip." So with a big smile on his face, Snuffles stepped outside the burrow into the sunlight and ran straight into his mothers waiting arms.

He started to followed his mother into town when all at once before they had gotten five steps down the path a big ruckus broke out from Snuffles' sisters and brothers. Mom turned and looked straight at Annabelle and said, "You are needed here to look after the little ones. Don't let them get into trouble while we're gone. Chip, help Annabelle. You know she'll need help. Today is Snuffles day. He's old enough to do this. Be good." and with a big smile she turned and took Snuffles' hand and they strode down the path towards town.

Annabelle, Chip, Hermie and Missy stared with their mouths open in disbelief as Snuffles and his mother headed down the path. Annabelle shouted, "I'll take care of them mommy. Don't worry. Have fun Snuffles."

As Snuffles and his mother rounded the corner he looked back to see his other siblings staring at Annabelle in disbelief.

Snuffles mother lead him down a different path towards town, one that he had never seen her use before. The little Hedgeling was instantly curious and started asking questions.

"Where are we going mother? This isn't your usual way into town." inquired Snuffles.

"Oh, I just thought I'd take the scenic route today. Is that OK with you?" she asked.

"Sure, I'm ready for anything," he told his mom, but as he said this to her his mind started to wander and as he followed her through the forest he was imagining danger at every turn. As they traveled deeper into the forest Snuffles attention turned more to what the forest actually looked and felt like.

The forest was cool and shaded with light filtering through the trees. The path into town was paralleled by a small creek with soft ferns and mosses that grew right down to the creeks edge.

"Wow, fish! Maybe Chip and I can come back and catch some." said Snuffles.

His mother laughed when she saw how excited he was. They played a while longer taking off their shoes and splashing or kicking in the water at each other. Mom looked up at the sun which had moved father into the west.

"It's getting late, we had better be getting to town or we won't have food for dinner tonight."

Snuffles wiped off his feet and put on his shoes. They were ready to head towards town.

Many of the forest locals know where the wild vegetables and fruits grow. Mom stopped and taught Snuffles how to pick onions, berries, mushrooms, herbs and fruits. They had one of their shopping bags almost full when they came upon a nest of eggs. Two hummingbird eggs are enough to feed their whole family. Snuffles mom also taught him about not being greedy in the forest. "Never take everything. The forest must replenish itself just like we do. We always leave what we don't need. She reminded him that by giving back there will always be more for the next time."

"What about the winters? We need more food to last when it snows and we can't get out to collect it."

"It's true that we store food in the winter but, we don't take more than our family will use. We don't want to waste. If we waste by taking too much what good would that do us or anyone else. We would throw it away in the spring because it spoiled and someone else that needed it would have gone without because of our greed."

"I see what you mean." said Snuffles.

They continued on down the path and all the way into town Snuffles asked questions about everything he saw. By the time they arrived in town Snuffles mother was just about to burst with laughter.

"I declare, I don't know when I've every met a little one with as many questions as you have. What's going on with you?" She asked him.

"I don't know. Everything is so wonderful and we've had so much fun I just don't want to miss or forget any of it." He replied. So together they went hand in hand all the way into the village. Snuffles felt so happy to be with his mother and was glad that she let this be his special day with her.

Chapter 5

Versailles

The little village of Versailles was very quaint and old fashioned and as Snuffles and his mother approached the village his mother walked more tall and proud than he had ever seen her. She made sure that she introduced her Snuffles to everyone she met.

Mrs. illuminating, who lived two doors down from the post office, was out watering her flowers when Snuffles and his mother arrived. She raved when she got a look at Snuffles and just about hugged the stuffing out of him when it was time to leave. She kept saying how he looked just like his mother and how proud she must be. Then there was Mrs. Corey who lived above the grocery store. She just smiled while mom talked and kept offering Snuffles cookies which he gladly ate. They were wonderful and she had just baked them so they were still warm which made them soft and gooey. The sneak attack happened when they were leaving, Snuffles was just about out the door when Mrs. Corey reached down and squeezed Snuffles cheeks so hard they went numb instantly. Snuffles made a special mental note right then and there to stay as far away from the cheek squeezing Mrs. Corey no matter how good her cookies were.

The village square was made up of many shops. There was a grocery store on the main corner that had so many smells as you walked by that you knew you had to walk in and shop for some of the mouth watering treats. The post office and city hall were built next to each other, when you looked at them from the street, the buildings looked like two mushrooms squeezed together. Versailles had great variety of shops, clothing, sporting goods, hobbies shops and even a restaurant. Every building in the town had its own unique design and look about it. The library was especially fun, when Snuffles and his mother walked in his eyes could not believe how many books were on the shelves. He spent the better part of an hour choosing books that he could take home and read to Hermie. But, the best place that Snuffles ever saw was the village park. The park was larger than anything Snuffles had ever imagined. There was a forest, a play area and climbing equipment. There were a lot of things for a family, or even one little Hedgeling to do.

Snuffles' mother told him to wait in the park while she went to the grocery store. This was so exciting to Snuffles. His mother was trusting him to be alone by himself for the afternoon. He knew he would now get to explore like the big kids did. Snuffles kissed and hugged his mom good-bye and watched as she left.

Chapter 6

The Hidden Cave

When he turned around he began to realize just how big his world had started to look without his mom being there to protect him. He also realized that it looked a bit frightening too. The park was big enough but the forest seemed to be drawing him into its thick and tangled weblike vines. Taking a deep breath Snuffles took off for a small forested area. As he approached the forest, he noticed that is was getting darker. There were so many over hanging branches from the trees up above that it felt like dusk. The forest seemed scary and inviting all at the same time. It made the quills rise on the back of his neck yet, his curiosity was getting the better of him. When he got there he followed the outer edge of the forest for a while until he bumped into another Hedgeling his same age. This boy seemed to be as tall as he was but had more black quills around his face than Snuffles had. Snuffles had not seen him before so he guessed that his home was outside of town. When Snuffles looked into his face and saw that he seemed to be as mesmerized with the forest as he was, he had to smile.

"Hi, my name is Snuffles. What's your name?"

"I'm Prickles," said the little hedgehog. "Have you been here long."

"No, this is my first time at the park. My mom is shopping and she dropped me off, so I got to be here and explore alone."

"Wow, my mom didn't let me out of her sight for at least two times before she would go off shopping. Boy, you're lucky."

"Have you been in the forest before?" asked Snuffles.

"No," he said. "But I've been trying to get brave enough to go in. I really want to know what's in there. This time I brought a lantern so I can see better and now that you are here maybe we can go together," replied Prickles with an odd grin, looking at Snuffles. Snuffles agreed and the boys set off apprehensively toward the dark edges of the forest.

The underbrush was thick and snagged their clothing as they entered along the overgrown path. Prickles had been in the scouts and taught Snuffles how to blaze a trail so as to not get lost. Each boy tried to mark the direction they were going by putting stones in little pyramids on the path about every 100 feet or so.

The eerie sounds of the forest creatures overhead had the both of them looking over their shoulders constantly. The forest path seemed to take so many turns that it wasn't long before they lost their directions altogether. Up ahead they could hear the sound of water running so they headed along the path towards it. They approached the small babbling brook that traveled through most of the forest and both Snuffles and Prickles let out a sigh of relief when the path got larger and easier to follow. They were relaxing after climbing through all the underbrush when Snuffles and Prickles settled down in a small clearing and kicked off their sandals to play in the brook. They started to talk and get to know each other. Their imaginations began to run away with them as they chatted about tales of ghost and pirates that had been passed down through their families. They were continuing farther up the path, when they noticed that the forest seemed to be growing darker by the minute, Snuffles was happy that Prickles had brought along a lantern. Coming to an outcropping of boulders they climbed up to a large shelf area that overlooked the brook. While they were standing there catching their breath, Snuffles turned around and spotted a cave surrounded by thick and scratchy bushes. Both boys cautiously approached the opening in the bushes.

"Wow, what a cool cave," said Prickles. "This could be our own secret place. We wouldn't have to tell anyone about it and we could meet here and do things in secret. I'll bet we could even get our families to let us camp here eventually."

Snuffles thought about it and agreed, "I think this could be a really fun place. We could fix it up real nice and it doesn't look like anyone has been here in years."

"Been here in years! Would you like to climb that rock every day to live here? I don't think so." said Prickles. Both the boys laughed and slowly started to clear away the bushes blocking the entrance to the cave.

Once the opening was cleared Snuffles and Prickles pulled out the lantern and lit it. They approached the mouth of the cave and started to explore. The entrance was barely big enough for one little hedgeling to fit into but once inside, the cave opened up into an enormous cavern room that would fit three of Snuffles burrows in it. Making their way up and down rock ledges they came to a room that had water running. Shining the lantern around they saw hundreds of stalactites and stalagmites. Snuffles whistled under his breath, "Wow, when it gets really hot this summer this is the place to come and cool off."

"That's a great idea and we can bring our food down here to store so it can stay fresh and cold." Prickles replied.

"The passage way to the next room is light maybe we should save some lantern oil and turn it off for the time being."

"OK, I think we can make it without getting hurt and we are getting a bit low on the oil," said Prickles shaking the lantern and looking down the reserve peep hole.

As they entered into the next room they were visited by a blast of fresh air blowing through the darkness and hitting them in their faces. On further inspection they noticed that in the top of the room there was a hole that lead to the outside and a small amount of daylight was coming through it. They stood there enjoying the air but could hear strange sounds coming from the outer edges of the room.

"Prickles I don't think we're alone. I feel like someone is watching us." Snuffles said in an extremely nervous voice.

"Who's there!" shouted Prickles. "Answer me!"

When no one said anything their nerves started to get the better of them and their quills started to rise. Prickles reached down and lit the lantern. Just when the flame was glowing brightly Snuffles picked it up to shine it around the room. The boys had hardly enough time to react when the room instantaneously burst into a flutter of screeches and screams. Both Snuffles and Prickles took off at a dead run for the door and the startled bats took off flying for the exit in the roof.

Outside the room both boys panting hard leaned against the cave walls until they could slow down their breathing and could think straight again.

"I think we should count this room as off limits," said Snuffles.

"No doubt about that! I don't want to even go near there again," Prickles replied.

After an hour or so they made it back to the front entrance. As both boys sat on the floor of the cave thinking and dreaming about what they planned to do they also thought about who might know about the cave. After careful consideration they decided that no one should know where they had been or anything about the cave. They decided to keep it a secret.

"Prickles, we both have sisters and I know that mine are very nosy. Let's make the first rule that no girls be allowed at the cave. That way we'll make sure they don't get in and mess things up for us."

"That sounds good to me," replied Prickles, "I don't much care for girls anyway, especially sisters. They're always causing me trouble!"

"Also, I think that for the time being maybe we shouldn't tell anyone about the cave, at least until we have it set up the way we want it.".

With that in mind both boys spent the rest of the afternoon playing and planning the things that they would do when they had it all fixed up. Snuffles and Prickles were just about ready to go back to the park when they heard their mothers calling. The boys looked up in surprise when they heard their voices so clearly.

"I didn't think we were this close to the park."said Prickles

"That means we'll have to be extremely careful not to let anyone follow us in here if we're going to keep it a secret like we want."

"Right, but for now I think we better high tail it out of here or we'll both be in big trouble." Said Prickles."My mom doesn't like it when I show up late for anything. Especially if she's been calling me for a while."

"I think you may be right."answered Snuffles."My mom doesn't get angry but if she tells Chip I'll be done in for sure."

The boys picked up the pace and raced through the woods to their mothers who were waiting at the edge of the forest. As they approached the edge both Snuffles and Prickles glanced at each other with a knowing look of dread thinking that their lives would be over. But instead their moms were there looking into the forest with their own knowing looks and smiles on their faces.

"Where have you been?" inquired Prickles mom in a rough, you're in trouble voice. But before Prickles could answer Snuffles mom chimed in.

"Now don't go making things up that will get the two of you deeper in hot water than you already are. Like you think the two of us don't know where you've been."

Snuffles and Prickles both looked at the ground wondering what to say next. Then Snuffles said,

"We went into the forest mom, its part of the park, I thought it would be alright. How did you know to look for us here?"

"Well in case you didn't know I grew up in this park too. I think I know just about every inch of the forest and all its wonderful places too. I don't mind you're going in the forest but I do want you to let me know if you are going there. In case something happens I want to know where to find you. Now we're late for getting supper on so let's head home." With that she turned, said goodbye to Prickles mom and was off down the road. Snuffles ran off to keep up with her when Prickles yelled.

"Bye Snuffles."

"Bye Prickles. Remember, we'll meet here tomorrow if it's OK," Snuffles yelled back and put his finger up to his lips to indicate to Prickles to keep their secret.

"OK," he replied as he waved goodbye to his friend.

Both Snuffles and Prickles ran off with their mothers, giggling all the way home anticipating how much fun they were going to have in their new secret place.

Chapter 7

I've Got A Secret

That night dinner was a total disaster. Snuffles couldn't sit still, thinking of all the fun that he was going to have with Prickles in their new hideout. He was so anxious about seeing Prickles the next day that everything he tried to do was wrong. Trouble followed him from the moment he got home until the time he went to bed that night.

Annabelle told him to set the table, he dropped two dishes that broke into what seemed like a million pieces. Missy was underfoot more than usual, and when he found her sneaking into his private box, he had slapped her hand, probably harder than needed. She immediately started to wail and that brought down the wrath of Chip. He had ordered him to sweep and mop the whole house before he could eat dinner. What a mess!!! When bedtime came and his mother came in to see him, she sat on the end of his bed and smiled.

"So, I see you've had a very busy day, Snuffles," she said, "I think that maybe that's why your head's been somewhere else tonight."

"I'm so sorry mom, I had such a great day and I made a great new friend. I guess I've been thinking too much about all the things we did. I really didn't mean to cause so much trouble. I won't let it happen again, I promise." mourned the little hedge-ling.

24

"Well when you remember to at least say your sorry, I can always overlook a few of the little things that happen. Helping with the family's work is very important to me. When we all work together things get done much faster and if you can just keep focused on you're jobs we won't have a lot of extra work." Snuffles mom looked at him with her eyes twinkling. "You've grown up so much these past few years. With school and now friends of your own I don't know where the time has gone. So, what big secrets did you and Prickles find playing in the woods today?"

Snuffles looked up at his mother and wondered how she could have found out about the hideout but remembered that she had told him she played there as a girl. Maybe she didn't know, or maybe she was just guessing. Snuffles knew he had to be very careful not to let on that he knew anything about a cave and still make sure he didn't exactly lie to his mom either. Rules were strictly followed in their burrow and being caught in a lie was a punishment that Snuffles didn't want to happen to him. He remembered how just last week Missy was caught telling a lie to Chip about where she had been and, boy, did she really get it. Snuffles didn't like the idea of telling a lie to his mom either, she had always trusted him and it didn't feel right misleading her. So he decided he just wouldn't tell her about all the things he did and that way he could keep his secret and be able to sit down, all at the same time.

"Well, when Prickles and I met we played for a really long time on all the play-ground equipment. I think I like that rocking bridge the best. After a while we went exploring and followed a path around the edge of the forest. It goes in where you saw us come out. That path takes you down to the bottom of the ravine and connects to the creek. We were throwing rocks in the creek when we heard you calling and came running."

Looking as if she was satisfied with his answer Snuffles breathed a small sigh of relief. "Now, I think that's just about enough excitement for two boys in one day, don't you think?" She asked.

"I think so, I'm really tired. Prickles and I are going to play in the park tomorrow if that's OK with you?" he asked.

"I think that sounds fine with me, but only after your schoolwork and chores are finished. I'm glad you found such a good friend to play with. I do have one really big rule and I want you to obey it. You are to be home by sundown. I get very worried when my children aren't home in the evening by dinner time. I would miss you too much if anything happened to you, do you understand?" she asked.

Snuffles nodded his head in agreement.

"OK, well goodnight." And with that she kissed him and left the room. Snuffles closed his eyes and fell right to sleep, all the while dreaming about the wonderful things that he and Prickles would do tomorrow.

That night Snuffles dreams were anything but peaceful. He and Prickles had turned the cave into a castle and the rock ledge in the front had become the drawbridge. All night long the two boys fought off marauders, fire breathing dragons and evil demons. They knew that they must protect the castle inhabitants and most importantly their families. By the time the next morning came Snuffles was more tired that when he went to bed the night before.

He padded his way into the breakfast room half dressed and looking worn out. Everyone was already dressed and eating. He had just started to eat his breakfast when Annabelle said.

"Boy, Snuffles you look sick. Maybe you should stay home today and get some rest."

Everyone at the table stopped what they were doing and looked straight at Snuffles. Normally having that said to you was a great excuse to get out of school but, Snuffles knew that if he didn't go today there would be no meeting up with Prickles afterwards so he replied, "Don't worry about me. I feel fine, really. I just had a busy night in the dream department."

Snuffles hurried and finished his breakfast and then headed to his room to finish getting dressed. Just as he was finishing brushing his teeth Chip yelled for him to get out-side so they could all head off to school. Snuffles ran through the kitchen, kissed his mom on the cheek and continued out the door to a slightly annoyed looking Chip who said.

"'Bout time," and slapped Snuffles on the back of his head. All the others started to laugh, even Snuffles. They were all giggling and chatting as they started down the path to school.

Chapter 8

School

The Versailles School was very unique. Kids came from not only the town of Versailles but from far away as well. Many of the connecting towns were at least six miles away. Not only did all the kids in the county go there but they were happy to go there. In their community going to school was a privilege and if you were lucky enough to go to school, you cherished it.

When you first arrived you thought you were looking at a block of marshmallows all stuck together. It was white in color and each of the square bricks had a pillow look about them. The building wasn't glossy but had a sort of satin sheen appearance to it. All the doors and window frames were cherry red and the front of the school was surrounded by flowering bushes of yellow and blue. The elementary, middle and high school were all put together in three connecting long buildings. The school was designed so that all levels could use certain rooms together without the cost of duplication, like the lunch room and the gym. There was a wonderful track, also football, baseball and soccer fields. The school offered many activities such as burrow building, languages, arts and hedgeling sports.

When Snuffles and his family arrived at school the sun was shining with just a few clouds in the air. Missy and Hermie both took off at a dead run to get to their classmates already playing on the play ground. They were both in the beginner grades.

Snuffles then went up to the middle grades. Even though he was the same age as Hermie and Missy he had passed out of the beginner grades a long time ago. After he was about ready to go in, Chip yelled a goodbye and he and Annabelle headed up to the high grades.

Hedgelings don't live by ages. There is no one to say if you're not six years old you cannot go to kindergarten. A hedgeling will be given a test occasionally and if ready will start school. Snuffles mom taught all of her children to read and write and do some math way ahead of most of the kids. So, when it came time to be tested they were more than ready for school.

The teachers were wonderful at helping kids to reach their goals. All of the staff made sure that there was no child that did without. Snuffles knew of teachers who even help kids get school supplies when their families couldn't afford them. Some would help kids to get coats and boots in the winter time. Snuffles both admired and loved his teachers. His family always set high educational goals for themselves and Snuffles was no exception, he found that science and reading were two of his favorite subjects.

When they arrived at school Snuffles' science teacher, Mr. Roberts, would always have different experiments for the class to do each day. He always challenged the kids to try new things. He liked it when they would give science a real hands on approach. Today's experiment was about crystals and how they were formed. Snuffles liked this experiment a lot because it helped him to under-stand how the stalactites and stalagmites were formed in the cave. Snuffles reading teacher, Mrs. Abbott, was fabulous. She would have the class read books out loud and then they took turns to act out the characters or they would build sets about the books that they read. The story they were working on now was about someone named Ruby. Ruby was being chased by dragons and that made this book one of Snuffles favorites. Even with all the fun things they were doing it couldn't stop Snuffles from day dreaming about the cave, and the fun that he and Prickles would have after school.

Chapter 9

Secret Treasure

*A*fter school, Snuffles asked Hermie to take his books home and then he went to meet up with Prickles who was already on his way to the park. They went back to their new hideout to see if it was as hidden as they thought it would be. As they walked down the path towards the cave they were careful to sweep away all the path markers that they had set up the day before. By the time that they had gotten back down by the brook they knew that no one would be able to find the cave. As they climbed up to the ledge in front of the cave they both plopped down overlooking the brook to catch their breath before the went in and started to unpack their belongings.

"It sure is pretty up here, don't you think?" asked Prickles.

"I was just thinking the same thing. It's also very quiet, you can hear things falling in the woods a long ways away." Snuffles said.

"Well if we don't get started we won't get done." said Prickles.

"Yep, and I promised my mom I'd be home before dark." Said Snuffles.

They started with the entrance, clearing and cutting away the scratchy vines until you could easily make out the doorway to the cave and they could climb through it without catching their clothing on it. Prickled was working very hard st something when Snuffles looked over and asked, "What're you doing?"

"I just thought I would . . ."and he held up a wreath made from the vine that spelled our welcome."I thought we could hang it over the door. My mom says it's good luck."he smiled.

Snuffles laughed, "I don't know about it being good luck but I think it's a nice idea. C'mon let's put it up."

The two worked at cleaning and clearing up the outside around the cave until it was just about time to go home. They stood back to admire their work and felt it as a job well done.

"Now that's a good looking cave entrance. Since we have this area looking so good tomorrow we can start on the inside." said Prickles.

"OK, I have a few things to bring that will help make the cave a bit more cozy."

"So, do I, and seeings how it's Saturday I can come early."

"I can too, that is as soon as my chores are done."

"Alright, I'll see you sometime tomorrow morning then."

"Ok, later."

They both headed out of the forest and waved to each other as they headed down their separate paths home.

The next day they were both at the cave early and began the task of setting up the burrow. In order to give their new found cave that lived in look Snuffles had brought two small campstools, an old wooden box that would serve as a table, a bag of his mom's chocolate chip cookies and a thermos of fruit juice. Prickles, on the other hand, brought some old tin dishes, lanterns and rugs for sleeping. As the boys worked on the final touches, Snuffles was using a shovel to level out the ground around the table when he hit something very hard in the floor. The harder he poked at it the more immoveable it seemed to be.

"Prickles, quick, come here I've found something," shouted Snuffles across the cave.

"What is it?"

"I don't know but it seems to be really big."

As both boys started to dig and scrape away at the ground they soon uncovered a large, rusty, rectangular tin box with what looked like seashells in-laid into the top and sides. The box was a quarter the size of the boys and on the front it had a very old lock, which was full of rust. In spite of the rust the lock, was still in good condition and held tight whatever was locked up inside. There wasn't a key to open the lock but the boys were dying of curiosity to find out what it held. They shook the box, hit the box, and they jumped on the box but it still would not open. Feeling very frustrated they decided they were going to need help if they were ever going to open it. Knowing that they couldn't ask their mothers because girls just were not to be allowed at the hideout they decided to take the box to Snuffles' Uncle Porcupine.

Chapter 10

Uncle Rufio Porcupine

Rufio Cornelius Porcupine is Snuffles' uncle. He was quite the ruffian as a lad thus earning him the name Rufio which he wore proudly and kept as his trademark name.

Rufio was taller and larger than most Hedgepeople but was considered by the locals as more of a gentle giant than a ruffian as his name and looks would make you think. Rufio lived in a burrow that was small in size but had many treasures from his adventures and travels to other lands. Uncle Porcupine had been in the Hedgehog Naval Unit and had traveled to different countries where he lived and learned about the people and their cultures. He would always tell Snuffles he was the Ambassador of Versailles and he liked to spread a little Ozark spirit whenever he could. So, when Snuffles and Prickles found their treasure, there was only one person Snuffles felt he could trust with its secrets, and that was Uncle Porcupine.

Snuffles and Prickles made their way through town dragging their newly found treasure chest on a home made sled that the boys had taken from Missy and converted for their own use. After about an hour of pushing and pulling the sled they arrived at Uncle Porcupines' burrow. It was late in the afternoon and threatening rain when both boys raced up the steps to knock on the door. When his uncle answered, the boys, in all their excitement, started blurting out the whole story as fast as they could.

"Hold on, hold on!" hushed Uncle Porcupine seeing that the boys were flushed with excitement. "Come in and sit down before the two of you have a heart attack."

The boys followed Snuffles' uncle into the kitchen were he poured them each a glass of milk and put out a plate of freshly baked June bug cookies, hot from the oven. After each boy had gobbled up half the plate of cookies and drank down the milk Snuffles' uncle turned to his nephew and said, "Ok Snuffles, let's have a look at what you've brought for me to see."

Snuffles and Prickles lifted their treasure box onto the table so that his uncle could examine it. Rufio looked it over very carefully, and after three or four minutes sat back, looked at his nephew and exclaimed, "Oh my, this is something very special, and from the looks of it very old. The lock itself looks to be at least a hundred years old. Were there any other clues or items buried with it to give you an idea as to what it is or who it belongs to?"

"No, we didn't find anything to help us try and figure out what's inside. I thought that it was too special to try and bust up, but we did hit the lock with the shovel and it didn't budge. Prickles and I were hoping that maybe we would get rich when we finally get it open. We thought that anything locked up this tight had to be worth a fortune. When we couldn't break into the chest, we hoped you could help us and we would split whatever was inside with you," said Snuffles with a twinkle in his eye.

Rufio thought about it for a moment, then told the boys he would be right back, he needed to go out back to the tool shed. When Rufio headed out the back of the burrow, he commented that if he was ever going to break into that chest he was going to need some very strong tools.

While he was gone, the boys had time to look around Uncle Porcupines burrow more closely. There were antiques and pictures everywhere. As Snuffles was looking at some of the pictures in the hallway, he came across a picture of his uncle and another add looking man in a military uniform, he was very different, almost like he was from another place or time. They were shaking hands and this fellow was holding an unusually decorated box that looked very old. The closer that Snuffles inspected the picture, the more sure he was that this fellow was giving the box to his uncle, his box, his treasure box, that is!

Right at that very moment the back kitchen door slammed, which startled Snuffles out of his concentration and he knew his uncle was back. He hurried back to the kitchen and met up with Prickles on the way. He quickly told him about his discoveries in the front hallway.

"Are you sure it's our box?" asked Prickles.

"Dead sure."

"Well, let's see what your Uncle has to say about it."

When they came into the kitchen Uncle Porcupine stood with a can of oil and some strange looking tools for trying to pry open the lock. The boys gave Rufio a peculiar look.

"What's the matter boys?" he asked.

"Well Uncle," stammered the little hedgelings, "are you sure that maybe the box doesn't look familiar to you?"

"Why would you ask that?" he inquired with a surprised look on his face. "I've never seen it before in my life."

"Are you sure?"

"Yes, why?"

"When Prickles and I went looking around your burrow, we found a picture in the front hall of you with another fellow holding an unusual box that looked very much like ours."

"You did? Show me where you saw the picture." Said Rufio.

Uncle Porcupine, Snuffles and Prickles all marched up to the front hall to take a look at it. When Snuffles pointed out the picture to his uncle he stared at it, a far away look came over his eyes.

"Uncle are you OK" asked Snuffles?

"Yes, yes," he replied.

"Do you remember the man in the picture?" asked Prickles.

"Well, that was a very long time ago and I haven't thought about him since the time we took that picture." Rufio's face took on a far away look, as if he was someplace else, then he started to tell the boys about when the picture was taken.

"I was in the Hedgehog Navy and we were sailing off the coast of Afrohedge Island. We came upon an unusual boat floating in the sea. The boat had a shape like a fish with colors that I had never seen used on a ship before. There was blue, pink and a sea green that when mixed together blended so well with the seas surroundings that we almost ran over the ship. As we pulled up along side the vessel we could see that the sails were crystal clear. At that time, the ship seemed adrift with no one on it. A few of the crew members and myself climbed on board to look around, I noticed that the ship had the look and feel of being very old. Down inside I could tell that it had weathered many a storm. I was about to go back to my ship when, I noticed a very unusual box sitting on the desk in the control cabin. I picked it up to look at it closely, It wasn't locked then, and I unlatched and opened the lid. When I lifted it the room started to glow all around me. It was so bright that it blinded me.

The next thing I remember, I woke up in a forest that was thick and lush and smelled very fragrant. I got up to look around and saw a very tall odd shaped building off in the distance. I stood there enjoying the complete silence and trying to get my bearings as to where I seemed to be, when I heard what sounded like horns approaching from the distance. The sound grew in such intensity, that, by the time it got close, it produced an earthquake of such magnitude that I could not stand upright for any length of time. With the ground shaking so violently, I got scared, and tried to move away from anything I thought might fall on me. I was heading for an outcropping of forest trees when suddenly a flash of lightning came from a nearby grove of trees off to my right. Several strange looking machines came out. They floated on air but had the appearance of odd colored fish. The men that rode in these machines looked like us but with some definite differences.

"What was that, Uncle?" asked Snuffles.

"Yea, how were they different?"

"Well first, instead of ears they had what looked like slits in the sides of their heads. Later I would learn they were gills for breathing underwater. There fingers and toes all had webbing that aided them in swimming. Their eyes had a clear protective eyelid that slid over the top when they entered the water. There were so many unique things to see. I eventually was allowed see a lot of their full magical powers."

"Go on Uncle, then what happened."

"The men on the machines formed a tight circle around me and cut off any escape that I might try. Their Captain came out to talked to me, but I couldn't understand any of the words he was saying. He ordered one of his men to do something and then with a small amount of commotion, one of the other guards brought out a device and placed it on my vocal cords and the temples on the side of my face. Once that was done, all of the sudden I clearly understood everything that was being talked about. The Captain and I talked for quite some time and I found out that their King, King Jerod, had been kidnaped by some unscrupulous pirates. They had found access to their world quite by accident, like I had done. They threatened the inner world by taking King Jerod hostage and escaping with him using his powers to transport them back to the outer world. The Captain told me that he feared for the Kings life and was afraid that he might be killed by the pirates. Without the King, who had no children, there were no Aires to take his place, so his power could not be passed on. This meant that their world would not be able to survive. I tried to reassure him that it could not be as bad as all that, but when I learned about the King and that he was the only one to have certain powers, I knew he must be returned to his people right away."

"The powers that King Jerod possessed controlled the environment and protected their universe and without his control, their world would start to flood and go dark. They would be vulnerable to attacks of all types from the ocean and the outer world. In essence, their world would perish."

"Even as I stood there talking, I could feel changes happening around me. The light surrounding me was not as bright and the air did not feel as fresh as when I had first arrived. I told their Captain that I wanted to help. If I could get back to my ship in the outer world I would search for their King and hopefully return him in time to save their world. Unfortunately, I was informed that without the Kings power the portal back to the ship would not work. The Captain explained that I would have to travel to the surface a very different way from the way I came to them.".

"Captain Heron, as I would later learn his name, and his men escorted me down to the docks where the people were feeding and caring for some of the most strange and wonderful sea creatures that I had ever seen. Every creature that I had been taught to look upon as a sea monster seemed to be living there. The most remarkable thing was that these creatures looked at their care givers with an almost loving and docile attitude. They lived in complete harmony with each other.""As Captain Heron led me farther into the dock area and past a heavily guarded doorway, there was a secluded warehouse. We entered through a large, odd shaped oval door where approximately 15 barnacle covered pod shaped machines were kept. They were so well disguised that by looking at them you would never have guessed that they were not a natural item from the sea. With the exception of a small portal sized window in the top, there seemed to be no doorway at all."

"This is the only way to the surface now," said Captain Heron.

"Laughing at the surprised and confused look on my face, the kindly Captain proceeded to fill me in on the operation of the vessel. He reached down and rotated a barnacle on the side below the window and with the push of a button the pod sprung open like a flower with large petals. I was frightened to learn that the pod would not take me all the way to the surface. When I reached within ten meters of break water, the pod would open and eject me toward the top. While it would slowly fill with water and silently sink back to the sea floor where they could retrieve it. The Captain told me that this was how they had maintained their secrecy for centuries before the portal on the ship had been developed. Unfortunately this meant that I would be stranded in the ocean with no boat. I was guaranteed that I would be within yelling distance of my ship. My only worry was that I hoped and prayed that they would hear my cries for help!

I shook Captain Herons hand and he wished me good luck and then I climbed into the cramped little space and they closed the hatch. It felt as if I was shrouded in a very small coffin with no way out. Swallowing my fears of panic and claustrophobia, I gave the thumbs up sign and felt the pod start to move. It slid down the ramp into the sea where it moved along the current towards the end of the bay.

As I sat there looking out the window, I could see the village surrounding the wharf, I marveled at the people looking back at me. They seemed not surprised by this very strange looking object floating past them. I could see all the sea creatures, both on top and below the surface, where I marveled at their enormous size. I was staring off into the distance, when I could feel the pod picking up speed. The next thing I knew the pod started to accelerate at a high rate. I was shooting quickly down a dark tunnel which was making the trip all the more frightening. The speed at which the little pod was traveling was amazing. I was literally pinned hard against the back of my chair where I could not even raise my head from the headrest. I looked out the window and all I saw was total darkness. This seemed to go on for what seemed an eternity when all of a sudden, whoosh! I felt the pod make a sideways slipping motion and come to a complete halt which nearly threw me onto the floor. Out my window I could barely make out the ocean with all its colors and life. Then the pod started to rise at a comfortably slow pace. I was watching the amazing amount of sea life at that depth and found myself awestruck at the beautiful colors and shapes before me. I noticed that the ocean seemed to be not as dark as before, so I guessed I must be close to the surface. I sat there for quite some time enjoying the ocean world before my sense of safety was replaced by complete and total terror as I realized that the pod had started to fill with water. Although my thoughts could make me think of nothing but drowning, I somehow managed to remember the instructions that Captain Heron had given me. I climbed up and stood on the stool in the center of the pod. When the pod had filled half way with water, I took a deep breath just as the pod burst open. I then felt myself being propelled towards the surface.

As I broke free from the world of darkness and into the world of sun and air I felt deliriously happy that I was, in fact, in sight of my ship. I swam toward it pounding the water as I went. I screamed and flailed my arms for what seemed like an eternity before I was finally seen by a crewman who threw me a lifeline and hoisted me aboard. Once I had dried off, I went straight to the Captain's cabin to update him on the pirates in the area and to let him in on what I believed happened to the crew of the vessel we found. I thought long and hard on how I was going to keep the King's information out of the conversations. I hoped to help by not telling my captain who he really was. I knocked on the door.

"Come in," said Captain Smith. "Well, Rufio I'm glad to see you didn't shrink when you fell into the water off that old relic."

"I must admit, Captain, I do feel a little bit like a prune."

"Well, I'm just glad you're OK. Are you here to make a report?".

"Aye, Captain." And with that I started to describe some of my findings, as to what I felt had happened to the crew. I told him that I thought the operator of the vessel had obviously been kidnaped and was probably on their ship being taken back to their home port.

"What makes you believe there was anyone on board that old derelict anyway," he inquired.

"Well, sir, there was evidence of dirty dishes in the sink with fresh food on them and I also saw unmade beds which lead me to believe that the ship was occupied. Now, as for a kidnaping, I saw some signs of what looked like a scuffle had taken place, but there was no blood."

"You would have made a fair detective, Lieutenant." Laughed Captain Smith. "OK, let's make sail into the trade winds and chase down these alleged culprits. With any luck maybe we'll be able to rescue the crew of that vessel before any harm can come to them."

"Aye Captain, right away!"

As I left the cabin, I breathed a sigh of relief that he had not asked me for any more information about the ships occupants. With any luck I might be able to keep my promise and help the King without revealing his identity.

As we filled our sails and turned into the trade winds we set a course along the route most commonly followed by pirates. I was amazed that the old derelict vessel seemed to be following us. It was as if it knew we were going to save its master. Everyone on the ship was beginning to feel a bit spooky by the occurrence. We had sailed for nearly two days when the derelict simply vanished. I don't know if I felt better that it was gone, or if I worried more because of it, nevertheless, the crew seemed to feel much better and that was the most important thing. All along the way we never caught site of any other vessels in the area. For such a common shipping route, it seemed to be totally devoid of any activity. Both the captain and I were beginning to worry that we might be on a wild goose chase, but by the time the sun was setting on the third day, we were approaching Yetahedge Island, known to be inhabited by some of the most rabid pirates around.

I, as well as the captain, assumed that this little island would probably be where the pirates had taken the crew and the King.

Through the cover of darkness we set anchor just off the northern tip of the island and quietly slipped our skiffs into the water. As we headed for shore we could hear loud noises coming from the community near a docking area approximately a half mile away.

"What happened next, uncle?"

"Yea, did you find the pirates or save the King?"

Uncle Porcupine looked at his watch and noticed that the sun had indeed gone down.

"Well, that will have to wait for another time. Right now I have to get both of you home or your mothers will be angry with me."

"But uncle!" Snuffles protested.

"Oh no," he hushed them "you know I'm right. Now let's get going."

With sad looks on the boys faces, they allowed Rufio to take them home. Prickles had already asked to spend the night at Snuffles, so they had only one stop to make. The boys went up the steps to go inside but turned to Rufio before going in.

"Uncle, you will finish your story tomorrow won't you? You won't forget again will you?" Snuffles asked with an inquisitive look on his face.

"Not to worry boys. Tomorrow we'll finish the story and open the chest together."

The boys waved a farewell to Rufio and then turned and went inside for dinner.

Uncle Porcupine waved back to the boys and then went back to his burrow. Once there, he sat at the kitchen table staring at the chest. Like the boys, he was dying of curiosity and it was getting the better of him. He picked up his tools and went to the chest. With a determined look on his face, he grasped the lock with his hand and as he lifted the lock toward him it slid open as if it had never been latched. Rufio held his breath as he started to lift the lid. At that same moment, the clock in the hall started to chime out midnight, which made Rufio look up and the quills on the back of his head stand up. He lifted the lid very slowly, not really sure what he was getting into, but knew he had to know and at the same time, that same eerie glow that he remembered from the first time, started. Then, without warning the lid slammed shut and Rufio was gone.

Chapter 11

Gone

After dinner, Snuffles and Prickles went upstairs to his room.
"That was the best Junebug meatloaf I've ever eaten, your mom can sure cook," said Prickles.

"Thanks. My mom makes really good food."

The boys played games and watched a movie but their conversation always came back to the chest. They discussed the story that Rufio had told them and wondered if it was true. They were speculating on the story's ending when Snuffles said,

"I can't stand it. After hearing about all the mystery surrounding the chest all I want is to know more than ever what's inside it."

"I feel the same way, but I don't know what we can do about it right now."

"I know a way we could find out after everyone has gone to bed."

"How's that?"

"We could go back to my uncles house," Snuffles said.

"Oh that's just fine and how many years do you think we'll be on restriction for that one?"

"I think if we're lucky, we might be able to get to my uncle's burrow and sneak in the back of the kitchen without being noticed."

"That sounds like a good idea I just hope we can pull it off. How do you plan to find out what's inside the box?"

"I'm not sure yet but I'll have that figured out by the time we get there. I think if we are really quiet Uncle Porcupine will never know we're there. Then we can take the chest out behind the old barn and open it. If all goes well, we would be back here and in bed before anyone knows we're gone."

"So far I'm liking this. If we don't get caught I think it just might work."

The boys planned the details on how they would sneak out of the burrow after everyone had gone to bed. That night seemed to go on forever. Finally Snuffles' mom came in to tuck them into bed and say goodnight. The boys waited patiently for the sounds of the family sleeping. Then as quietly as they could, they snuck down the stairs and out the door into the night.

The boys shut the door without making even the slightest sound and then went down the porch stairs. They paused to listen to the sounds of the night. The secadas buzzed loudly while the frogs were singing down by the creek. The night was dark but had a clear crisp feeling about it as you stared up at the stars. They were so focused on trying to be quiet, that neither boy noticed that they were being watched. As they went out the door a figure in the shadows stood very still watching and waiting.

Snuffles and Prickles grabbed the flashlights that were hidden in the bushes by the back door and hurried down the path through the woods. The path leading to Uncle Porcupines burrow had many curves and at night made travel, at times, a little scary. The trees with their moss hanging down waved with the slight breeze and gave a ghostly appearance at every curve. When they finally arrived at the burrow they noticed that the light was on in the kitchen. Both Snuffles and Prickles stood staring at the back door wondering what to do next. A feeling of confusion came over them as they both looked at their watches and saw the late hour. Why was Uncle Porcupine still up? Snuffles knew that his Uncle usually went to bed very early. He thought it was because he was such an early riser. Snuffles always thought it was a routine he had gotten into from his years in the Navy.

to find out what the mystery was all about. He went to the table and picked up the chest and was about to open the lid when the screen door flew open and in burst the boys.

"Stop!"They yelled in unison.

The figure stopped and slowly turned to look over at the boys.

"Hermie?! What are you doing here?" shouted Snuffles.

"I wanted to know what you and Prickles were up to and where you were going so I followed you here," he replied.

"So that was you outside with the boxes?" Prickles asked.

Hermie nodded.

"You really scared us!"

"Sorry I didn't mean to, but it was the only way I could see in the window to find out what was going on." He replied shyly.

"We're not doing anything that concerns you. Now go home!" said Snuffles.

"I don't think so. I think I'll just wake up Uncle Porcupine and tell him you're stealing his stuff." The little hedgehog stood there with his arms crossed and both feet planted firmly on the ground glaring at his brother as if daring Snuffles to move him.

Snuffles took a deep breath and finally said,"Haven't you figured it out yet? With all the noise that's happened, our uncle hasn't come in. We don't know what's happened to him. He's disappeared."

Hermie stood there silently for the first time, thinking about what his brother had said. With a strange look on his face, he made his decision. He looked straight into his brothers eyes, picked up the chest and threw the lid wide open. The room started to glow with such a bright light that it became blinding. All three squinted their eyes straining to see into the light. It felt as if someone had poured itching powder all over their skin and then they were gone.

Chapter 12

A New World

Rufio awoke smelling sweet grasses and fragrant flowers surrounding him. As he opened his eyes, he stared into the face of his long time friend King Jerod.

"What are you doing here?" asked Jerod.

"I'm not quite sure," answered Rufio.

Rufio quickly told King Jerod about the events leading up to his arrival. The whole time his friend listened quietly. After contemplating the information from him Jerod asked Rufio in a soft voice, "Do you remember how you got the chest?"

"No, not really. When the boys found the picture of the two of us in the front hallway of my burrow, I started to remember some of the events that led up to finding you. I don't really remember a chest."

"Rufio, I gave you that chest when you rescued me from the pirates. Your shipmates and Captain were given wishes as a reward for saving me. Most of them have used theirs by now. I knew you had worked harder to protect my world and my identity, than any loyal subject could ever be expected to. There was not enough gold in the world to repay you for your efforts. You surprised me even further by your humbleness. You refused compensation for your help. So, I gave you a gift instead, the chest. I placed a special enchantment on it."

"What did the enchantment do to me?" Rufio demanded.

"It didn't do anything to you, but instead, my gift was to give you another life. The chest enchanted you to hide it somewhere special and then make you forget about it until you reached an age that would mean your time in the outer world would be over. Somehow, something went wrong, we never anticipated on children finding the chest. But, I do find it extremely curious that it was your nephew that found it."

"How would the chest know my time was up in the outer world?" asked Rufio.

"We have very special powers that can predict these events. I mixed them with the enchantment so it would recognize that your time was at hand. The enchantment would then take over and lead you, and in this case your nephew, to uncover the chest. Once you had the chest back in your possession and opened it, you would be transported back to my world here. I would be sent a signal, as I was when you came, to greet you. Here is where we must sort out if your time has come or not. This is where time stops and you never age or change. Those, that are very old, are sent to the breath of steam to be purified and revitalized." Seeing the questioning look on Rufio's face he explained further. "The breath of steam is a special place that is like your Fountain of Youth, it can actually take years off your life."

"But, Jerod, the lock did open by itself when I touched it. The boys fought with it all day long and weren't able to break it open." said Rufio.

"That is very interesting, the lock would have only opened if it was your time."

"How can that be? I've never been sick, or hurt, or even had a bad day, in my life. Do you think that possibly the boys finding the chest started a chain of events that might have brought me here by mistake.

"I'm not sure about what events have happened and why. I'll have to talk with the high priestess to see if she has any answers to this problem. What I do know, is that the lock would only open for you and that instead of you finding the chest, your nephew found it. I am thinking that maybe it might have been right."

Seeing the confused look on Rufio's face he continued, "Rest assured, my friend, we'll get to the bottom of this."

"We'll need to do this right away. I don't want to give up my life just yet if I don't need to. I wonder what went wrong. I'm happy to stay here when it's my time. I can't think of a better place to live out eternity but I just don't think I'm through with the outer world yet." Explained Rufio.

"OK, I'll go see the high priestess right away. Rufio, be prepared when things get put into motion, sometimes, no matter how much we want, we can't reverse them."

"What would happen then?"

"You would remain with us here and take your place among the inner people."

"What if I don't want to give up what's left of my life just yet."

"Even if you are tied to us here, there are special ways that will allow you into the outer world for short periods of time," replied Jerod.

"Really!? Well, if I could still go back to the outer world on occasion I guess I could learn to live with a few restrictions,"thought Rufio out loud.

The King left Rufio to go see the high priestess, which allowed Rufio time to go explore and rediscover what might be his new world. He had a lot of questions to ask and a lot of them were about his basic needs. Rufio was following a path that lead down towards the bay area, when off in the distance he could heard the familiar sound of horns. He knew that someone had gone through the portal. Curiosity getting the better of him, Rufio followed the sounds and arrived in a small clearing with inner guardsmen and their machines encircling three boys.

"Snuffles, Prickles and Hermie!!"cried Rufio, as he raced forward to protect and rescue them from the menacing looking guardsmen. Seconds seemed to turn into hours as they stared into each others faces. A noise from the nearby forest shifted everyone's gaze and out walked Captain Heron. When the Captain approached his eyes met with Rufio's and softened a bit as he realized who it was.

"Well doesn't this seem to be a fine kettle of worms you've gotten yourself into Rufio. Why are you setting off my alarms and upsetting everyone. Great gods who are these lads?" he asked.

The boys tugged at their uncle's sleeve and Snuffles asked,

"What are they saying and how are you talking back to them Uncle?" That was when Rufio realized that he no longer needed the device to understand what was going on. Somehow he had indeed changed.

Rufio talked to the Captain and asked if the listening and talking devices could be used on the boys and if they could use them. The Captain agreed and he ordered the devices be placed on each of the boys and adjusted to their individual vocal patterns.

Rufio was still in shock as the boys tried to explain the chain of events that had brought them to the inner world. He knew for certain that the boys had opened the chest because little Hermie was standing there still holding onto it. Captain Heron seeing that he and his men were obviously not needed spoke. "Well Rufio, I can see that you have control of the situation and won't be needing us. We'll be heading back to the castle now." Looking straight at the three boys he said in a stern voice, "The King has a strict policy about intruders and visitors to our world. He will be wanting to see you right away. I think maybe we should escort you to the castle with us."

Rufio sighed and agreed with Captain Heron and they turned to head along the main road up to the castle with the boys in tow.

Chapter 13

Loggerhedge—
Evil of the Underworld

The boys were lost in thought and chatting like little birds on the way to the castle which made Rufio laugh to himself. Their excitement about the inner world had him looking back on how he must have looked to the guards and Captain Heron when he had first arrived. The boys had stopped on the side of the road and were giggling at what looked like a rabbit. It was quite purple in color with grey whiskers and paws and had ears twice the size of its body. Hermie had picked a flower and was bent over the bunny to feed it when a giant hole popped open below his feet and he disappeared kicking and screaming as he dropped out of site. The Guardsmen ran for the hole with their spears drawn and tried to catch Hermie but it was too late, there was nothing but thin air and screams. Rufio and Captain Heron grabbed a spear from the nearby guardsmen. Took a deep breath and jumped down the hole after Hermie.

They fell for what seemed an eternity down a dark tunnel which had both Rufio and Captain Heron tumbling and banging against the sides of the walls. When at last they landed it was with a hard thud in a pile on top of each other at the bottom of the shaft. Rufio stood up and started brushing the dirt off his clothes and looked over at Captain Heron who was now laying flat on his back coughing out big clouds of dust with each breath. Rufio asked Captain Heron, "What was that thing that grabbed my nephew?"

"That, was a Loggerhedge."

"What in the world is a Loggerhedge?"

"Only one of the most dangerous creatures that reside here in the inner world. The Loggerhedge dig incredibly fast and can pop up anywhere at anytime. They can smell our young and when they do they hunt them down. When a Loggerhedge takes a youngling we usually find only pieces of what is left of them."

Rufio's eyes widened to where they looked as if they might pop out of their sockets. Panic washed over him like a tidal wave and he felt as if he wanted to scream but their was no air in his lungs.

"I tell you now that I will not be bringing home pieces of my nephew. Do you hear!?" shouted Rufio in a menacing tone, "I am not willing to give up hope and seeing how you followed me down this hole I think we had better get started looking for him. The faster the better!"

Captain Heron stood up and handed Rufio a spear and both men lit a torch. They silently headed down the nearest corridor. The walls of the tunnel shone brightly and reflected the light from the torches with a strange illumination. They traveled around curves and corners and through rooms that were large enough for gatherings of over a hundred Loggerhedge people. The further they traveled the passageways the more dread that settled in the pit of Rufio's stomach. It was quiet, deadly quiet and there was no sign of Hermie. Where could he be? They had traveled another five minutes or so when Captain Heron reached out his hand to stop Rufio and there as they listened in the quiet they could hear muffled sounds off in the distance. Both men extinguished their torches and proceeded along the corridor in the now near darkness. Up ahead they could see the faint glow of lights which were getting brighter as they got closer to the source. Rufio felt a sigh of relief wash over him when he heard the sound of his nephew sobbing.

Hermie was surrounded by nervous looking stick people that looked as if they had moss stuck all over their bodies. The loggerhedge clan were of the oldest cannibalistic tribes existing in the inner world. Their tribes had been known to eat each other as a source of power. In days gone by the tribes had changed to eating younglings because of their purity. It represented the ultimate power to the tribesman who captured one.

As Rufio stared around the cavern he was shocked to see the reasons the walls were glistening. In one corner of the cave was a pile of youngling bones approximately fifteen feet high and an old woman who was very ancient looking. She was shorter than most of the Loggerhedge people and was stooped over. Her skin was gray and drawn and had the look of flaps of leather waving in the breeze. Her bones protruded at every angle and her moss like hair flew wildly around her face. She was missing almost all of her teeth so her mouth looked like a gaping hole. The eyes seemed devoid of any life at all. This evil old woman was grinding the little bones of younglings into powder and depositing them into a boiling cauldron of foul looking gruel. There were three or four servants there to take the mixture from her. They then proceeded to paint the walls of cavern with it. Rufio was throughly sickened be the sight of what was going on and wondered how this could still be happening in today's times. Still the reality existed that the Loggerhedge tribesmen had his nephew and if he wasn't very careful they were going to eat Hermie and possibly kill both of them.

Captain Heron and Rufio both figured that considering the Loggerhedge were very superstitious that a diversionary tactic could possible work to their advantage. They both crept around the back of the chamber carefully trying not to bump into anything that might alert the Loggerhedge to their presence. As they got closer to the old woman they noticed that she seemed to be blind.

"This could be just what we need to get your nephew back," whispered Captain Heron.

At that very moment the quills stood up on the back of Rufio's neck telling him he was not alone. He quickly grabbed his spear and spun around ready to attack but instead was confronted by Snuffles and Prickles. Filled with instant horror at the site of the two boys Rufio roughly grabbed them by the shoulders and lead them from the room.

"What do you think you were doing following us down here?" cried Rufio in exasperation.

"There was no one else to help, Uncle! They didn't even try." wailed Snuffles, "He's my brother, I've got to help him."

Rufio stared into the eyes of Snuffles and realized that this young man had the heart of a lion and that made him want to burst with pride at the man he was becoming. He reached out to Snuffles and gave him an affectionate hug.

"So you shall my great nephew and so you shall," said Rufio looking down into Snuffles deep brown eyes. "Captain Heron, you said that you had come up with a diversion. Can you fill us in on what we can expect?"

Captain Heron turned his head sharply toward Rufio at the mention of his name. His eyebrows deepened as he started to outline his plan for attack and how he thought they could free Hermie. "Well, you see that old woman over there, the blind one?" They all nodded. "I think that if we use the boys as a decoy by putting them upwind from her, she might just set off the alarm if she smells them."

"Wait a minute!" exclaimed Rufio throwing up his hands to halt all thoughts about where the conversation was going. "No one is going to put these boys in danger. There has to be another way."

"Uncle," said Snuffles softly, "You know that Captain Heron is right. I don't mind being the decoy if its going to help get Hermie back."

Looking into Snuffles and Prickles faces and seeing them both nodding in agreement Rufio knew that Captain Heron was right. "OK, what's next Captain?" he asked reluctantly.

"When the old woman sounds the alarm all eyes and bodies should be looking and heading towards the boys. Hopefully before she goes off we will be up against the cave walls around the backside of her and downwind. Then when everything is happening towards the boys, we can run up and dump that cauldron over on a few of the Loggerhedge people. That should distract the men into looking our direction. If we can get them to advance on us, and we are quick enough, the boys will hopefully escape unhurt. They can run to Hermie and help free him."

"This all sounds very good but, what happens if it goes wrong?" asked Rufio. "Do we have another plan?"

"I'm sorry Rufio, but that is plan one and two." Captain Heron said with lowered eyes.

"That's alright Mr. Porcupine sir," said Prickles, "because Snuffles and I are real fast and I know that we'll be able to get away from anything those loggerhedge people throw at us."

"That's right, we'll make you proud and I bet we'll get Hermie free too. One thing though?" He asked.

"What's that Snuffles?"

"You will make sure that you and the Captain won't get hurt or captured either. Won't you?" He asked with his big eyes glistening.

"Never you worry son. The Captain and I will be just fine. So if think that the two of you are ready, how about we get started on our plan to free Hermie. From the looks of him I think he's getting really uncomfortable." Said Rufio and everyone agreed.

Everyone turned to look over at Hermie who had a look of discomfort but seemed to be trying to put up a front of bravery. Both Snuffles and Prickles crept silently around the back of the walls of the cave being very careful to not get upwind of the old woman. Their goal was to not let her catch their smell until everyone was in position. As Snuffles and Prickles got closer to Hermie, Snuffles picked up a small pebble and tossed it gently toward him so as to alert him to their presence. Hermie startled at the noise and looked in the direction from where it came. As he squinted into the darkness he could just barely make out the outline of his brother. In his excitement he started to yell towards Snuffles but was quickly hushed by him. Snuffles had put his fingers to his lips to show Hermie how important it was to be silent but he also pointed a finger toward their uncle to let him know that help was on the way. Hermie gazed in the direction that his brother pointed and Snuffles and Prickles could see an instant sigh of relief wash over him.

Captain Heron and Rufio felt their way down a dark passage until they were directly behind the old woman. As they looked across the room they could see that the boys were in position. Captain Heron looked over at Rufio and asked, "Are you ready?"

"I'm as ready as I'll every be," gulped Rufio and he looked over at the boys. Rufio couldn't help but notice the fear in their young eyes. No one should go through this he thought. Snuffles looked over at him and he tried to give him a reassuring smile, they nodded that it was time to make their move.

The boys moved forward into the cave and the old woman put her head in the air sniffing, she suddenly let out a cry. As all eyes turned to her and she yelled "Younglings! Over there. Get em!" But the same time that she bellowed both Captain Heron and Rufio charged at the old lady shoving her aside as they ran straight for the cauldron. They grabbed the handles on the sides and lifted with all their might. Rufio glanced into the cauldron and noticed that it was a vile slurry brewing in the pot had an odor that was worse than any skunk he had smelled. Captain Heron looked straight into Rufio's eyes and nodded in the direction they were going.

At the top of the platform, where the old woman had worked approximately four feet above everyone else, the men noticed a large congregation of loggerhedge people staring at the boys. Rufio and Captain Heron poured the concoction over the nearest group. The cries from the group could be heard throughout the cavern and helped to refocus the loggerhedge on them. The clansmen throughout the cave rushed in to help the hurt and wounded people leaving Snuffles and Prickles alone and able to make a break for Hermie.

As clansmen started to run towards the injured loggerhedge, Snuffles and Prickles breathed a sigh of relief.

"I thought we were going to be caught for sure." whispered Prickles.

"We're just lucky so far. Come on let's get Hermie and get out of here before they see what we're up to."

They moved out of the shadows and into the cave all the while keeping their eyes on the war breaking out with Captain Heron and Uncle Porcupine in the center of it all. When they got over to Hermie he started to tell them all about his adventure, but Snuffles hushed him quickly.

"Wait till we get outta here, Hermie. We're not out of the woods yet."

The boys untied Hermie and quickly lifted him out of the cauldron, which was starting to get very warm. Grabbing him under his arm they started to run towards the cave entrance by dodging in and out of the shadows along the outer edges of the walls. As they ran Hermie's short little legs were barely touching the floor because of the grip that Snuffles and Prickles had on him. They were nearly lifting him off the ground.

Rufio's mind filled with instant fear as he realized that hundreds of loggerhedge were now racing towards them with their spears out ready for the kill. As he stood there frozen in time Captain Heron grabbed him by his shirt and spun him around. He focused on the Captain's face and he yelled, "Run!" They took off like lightning knocking over as many Loggerhedge as possible while they ran for the cave entrance. They grabbed the spears of the men as they fell over and quickly made their way to where the boys would hopefully be waiting.

The boys had already gotten to the archway and were well secluded out of sight. They peered around the edges of the arch watching the macabre display happening before their eyes. Snuffles uncle was performing miraculous feats of battle, the likes from which Snuffles had never seen before.

Rufio had been in many scuffles in his life and some that had depended on his cunning and intellect to get him out alive, but this was in no way like anything he had ever gotten into before. He and Captain Heron were only about half way through the cavern and were being attacked from all directions. Rufio knew that they were in real trouble and was about to start looking for a way to retreat out of there when he heard cries from up above their heads. Without time to think about what was happening overhead a wave of Hedgepeople descended upon them from a shaft in the ceiling Rufio ducked his head and grabbed as many spears as he could from the floor. It didn't take long to find out what was going on. A commotion broke out among the Loggerhedge and the fighting seemed to take a turn for the better. The Loggerhedge were preoccupied with something coming in from behind. All at once the room broke into a fiery glow that illuminated the cavern as bright as daylight. The Loggerhedge people having lived most of their lives underground, have very sensitive eyes and most were running for the cover of darkness while shielding their eyes. The noise that followed was thunderous and made the cavern vibrate with such intensity that Rufio felt as if he would shake apart. As the Loggerhedge took off running a familiar sound came from the entrance of the cavern. Captain Heron's guards had come in full force with their weapons drawn and were making short work of the Loggerhedge. Those that had not escaped or run away now lay all about the cavern floor.

The guard knowing that Captain Heron would be in serious trouble had gone immediately to the King to inform him as to what was happening. The King sent his special military unit of molehedge guard to create a tunnel down to the underground caverns of the Loggerhedge people. The molehedge people look exactly like Hedge-people with some exceptions. They have cupped feet and hands that make it easier for them to dig with. They have ear flaps on the side of their heads that lie flat so as not to get dirt in their ears. The can dig straight into the ground at an alarming speed and can make tunnels faster than anyone can using equipment. With tunnels being created by the molehedge the Kings guard were able to descend into the tunnels to help Captain Heron and hopefully save the civilians. Once inside the tunnels they quickly made their way along the dark passageways down to the cavern where they found the boys hiding. As the guard looked into the cavern from the archway it gave the appearance of what looked liked a war of the worst kind. People and body parts seemed to be flying in all directions. As they followed the trajectories of flight their eyes came to rest on Captain Heron and Rufio in the center of the cavern holding their own against a multitude of Loggerhedge people. The guardsman looked at Snuffles and asked, "All you alright?"

"We're alright sir, but can you help my Uncle. I don't think that he and Captain Heron can hold out for much longer."

"Well we'll see about that young man." answered the guardsman and without anything else being said he looked towards his fellow men, gave a quick silent nod and pointed in the direction of Rufio and Captain Heron. What happened next happened very fast because all of the guardsmen went flat on the ground and seemed to slide on their belly's along the walls of the cavern. Once they had encircled the Loggerhedge, three guardsmen stood up and shot flares into the air. They ignited and illuminated the cavern brighter than daylight. The phosphoreus smells burned your nose and made you gasp for breath. Many of the loggerhedge started to run away at that time. The guards-men all started blowing horn and whistles which was frightening in itself but those that did not run away found that they were outmatched and unprepared for the assault that was now reigning down upon them. Once the guardsmen made their way to Captain Heron and Rufio a look of relief came into their eyes.

Captain Heron looked over at the guardsmen and a smile appeared on his face, "What took you so long? I almost thought you were going to miss the party," he asked.

The guardsman started to laugh and was shaking his head, "Well, it looked to me like you had everything well in hand. I didn't think you needed us."

"I guess that just goes to show you that you shouldn't think so much," he bantered. "Rufio, I would like to introduce you to my brother, Felix." smiled Captain Heron.

"A great pleasure to meet you," replied Rufio huffing and puffing with exhaustion. "I don't care if your brother here wanted to party without you, I'm still very glad you showed up to this one. I don't think I was much help to him. I think he could have used a few of his fellow guardsmen." Rufio sighed. "Now if you both will excuse me I think I had better go check on the boys."

Rufio headed for the entrance to the cavern and after a short search found the boys surrounded by guards. Everyone seemed to be in good shape and the guardsmen looked as if they had adopted the young hedgelings as their mascots. As he approached the group the boys looked up at their uncle for a moment and then Snuffles ran into his arms. After a burst of hugs he released his Uncle.

"Oh Uncle we were so worried about you," cried Hermie, "I thought that you and Captain Heron were goners for sure."

"Not to worry, you're brother and Prickles had it all worked out. Didn't they Captain Heron?" asked Rufio looking over at the Captain who had just entered the room.

"Right you are. These are some of the bravest lads that I have ever had the pleasure to work with."

"Oh Mr. Porcupine sir, we didn't really do that much." said a quiet Prickles.

"On the contrary. Prickles, you and Snuffles did exactly what Captain Heron told you to do. You followed the orders that Captain Heron gave you and did them as well as any grown up would have done." explained Rufio. He looked over at Snuffles who had been quiet up untill now. "Why are you being so quiet, Snuffles,"

"I don't know. I guess I was just thinking about everything that has happened. I also, kind of feel sorry for the Loggerhedge people. I don't understand why they don't try to become friends,"

"I don't know the answers to that but maybe someday we'll find out."said Rufio."Anyway, I think we should get the three of you outta here and head home before anything else happens to us.

They all agreed and headed up the tunnel back to the surface.

Chapter 14

Safe Again

When they reached the surface everyone squinted at the bright light in their eyes. As they emerged from the cave entrance they were surrounded by the joyous sounds of all the village people who had come to take up vigilance at the entrance, awaiting the safe return of the men. Many of the villagers came up and patted them on the back. Emergency people were there to give assistance to their cuts and bruises. Little Hermie was the one in most need of the emergency help. He had bruises upon bruises and second degree burns on the lower half of his body. The people took him to a special hospital right away to attend to his needs. The guardsmen were greeted by their families and as Rufio looked around all he saw was love in the air. He couldn't help but think that all is right in the world and he was glad to be here and part of it.

Rufio started to look for Snuffles and Prickles and found they had slipped off together. When he found them he noticed they were by themselves. "What's up with the two of you," he asked.

"Prickles and I were just thinking about what's going to happen to us now that we're back here and what about you? What will happen to you?"

Prickles spoke up, "Yeah, I was just telling Snuffles that I want to go home and tell my mom about all the things we've done."

"When do you think that the King will let us get back to our homes?" Snuffles asked.

At that moment Captain Heron approached to talk to Rufio. "Um, can I have a minute of your time Rufio?"

"Sure, what is it,"

Captain Heron shuffled his feet for a moment and then said, "Alone, sorry boys,"

"OK, we'll be right back," Rufio said to the boys while giving the Captain a curious look. He and Captain Heron took a walk down the road towards the village.

After a long silence between them Rufio gave his friend a hard look and asked, "I think I'm getting to know you by now. What's on your mind?"

"Well before all this started we were on our way to see the King and he has informed me that I must bring you to him right away. I don't think, from the sound in his voice, that these are going to be the answers you want to hear."

"Don't worry, my friend, I think I've known for along time what the answer is and I've come to terms with whatever fate has dealt me. My only worry is for the boys at this time. They are needed at home with their families. They should be growing up in a safe environment playing with their friends, not fighting for their lives. The King has given me a wonderful opportunity to further my life and be useful. I suppose I'll never know the true reason that the box decided to open when it did and I don't know where it will take me but the adventure has had a wonderful start and a good outcome so far." As Rufio talked he got a far away look in his eyes but continued. "I will surely miss my family more than you can ever know but, I think I'm going to enjoy learning about my new family here as well." Rufio reached up and put his strong arms around his friends shoulders and gave him a squeeze. Both men looked at one another for a moment and smiled. They both traveled on in silence each lost in his own deep thoughts.

About a half a mile up a steep and winding road they came upon the castle. Rufio had never been this close to a castle before and stopped just to admire its beauty. The castle had long towers on each of its four corners that glistened in the light. It was cast in a bright white and had a purple tint to it. The flags on all of its towers were waving in a slight breeze. They were met by the castle guardsmen and escorted up to the Kings gathering room where he did his daily business.

When they entered the King's business chamber, both men walked up to the King and bowed.

"Please rise," said King Jerod, "I'm so glad that the two of you are alright. How are the boys?"

"They're fine," said Rufio, "I think Hermie will be in the infirmary for a while, but I think when all is said and done he'll have quite a tale to tell."

When Rufio said that, he noticed the Kings expression took on an odd look. "Don't tell me that the boys can't leave here either? What's going on Jerod?" Rufio demanded.

"Well," Jerod hesitated, "I went to talk to the High Priestess as I told you I would and she confirmed my suspicions. You were meant to be here with us at this time. The boys on the other hand present a very special problem. I agree with you that they need to go home to their families but I can't just sent them back with the full knowledge that they have of our world. As it is I have spoken with the infirmary and they have informed me that Hermie will need to stay their for at least another three days before his wounds have healed."

"So you're telling me that, there will be another three days of exposure to this world? How are you planning to keep this quiet?" Rufio asked.

"As you will come to learn we have a lot of magical powers in our world. We have been able to move people and time for thousands of years. We have a time machine that has been used in times of need that can displace and transport." and with a thoughtful look on his face he smiled at Rufio, "and if there where ever a time that it was needed I think it's now."

"Just how does this work?" asked Rufio, "Will it be safe enough to send the boys back without harming them, and what about me? What will happen to me and how will they explain my disappearance?"

"Hold on, don't go getting so upset before we've even had a chance to work out all the details. Hermie won't even be ready to leave the infirmary for three days and at that time I think we will have a plan to send them home safely. You see Rufio, time has been changed, as we have moved through time here so have their families. They think you and the boys have come to some sort of demise and have possibly met up with some fatal end as of this moment. What we have to create is the boys return just prior to all of this happening and we must come up with an escape for you that will satisfy every-one's questions."

"OK, I'll wait with the boys." And with a curt nod Rufio turned around and headed out the door to go and find the boys, mumbling all the way.

"Sir," Captain Heron started.

"Yes Captain what is it?"

"If I may ask a question?"

"Yes, go on." the King prompted.

"Sir, I would like to make the transition for Rufio as easy as possible. He loves Snuffles and his brother very much and I know he is especially fond of Prickles. Will there be any way for them to keep in touch after we send the boys home? I think he would be rather lonely if he couldn't see his family ever again. I know I would." Captain Heron spoke with a somber tone.

"I don't want you to worry. I think that everyone is concerned about Rufio and we want him to make a good adjustment to our way of life. Everyone in our world has a purpose and we'll be working to make sure that Rufio's purpose will challenge him both physically and mentally. But as to keeping in touch with his family I can see the importance in that and I will have to discuss with my advisors as to what, if any, thing can be done.

The Captain thanked the King for his time and turned to leave. He wanted to catch up with Rufio before he got too far down the road and try to smooth over his fears before he talked with the boys.

Chapter 15

The Village of Atlantishedge

S nuffles and Prickles watched as Uncle Porcupine and Captain Heron walked away up the road towards the castle. "I'll just bet they're talking about us. What do you think Prickles?"

"Yep, I can feel my ears burning already. Hey, I've got an idea. Since they're going to be tied up talking for a while why don't we go and check this place out on our own."

"That sounds better than sitting here waiting for them to come back. If I'm going to be sent home I want to see as much of this place as I can." Both boys stood up and started down the path towards the bay. "I think that the marina is over there. Let's go see if we can find the flower pods that Uncle Porcupine told us about. The ones that took him to the surface." said Snuffles.

"That could be fun. Your Uncle Porcupine talked so much about the animals in the bay I can't wait to see them." said Prickles.

They both headed off to the marina to explore and as they passed by the village shops they were amazed at how they looked so much like their own village. The bakery made both boys stop in their tracks as they smelled how wonderful it was. They were standing there staring into the front window not realizing, until now, just how hungry they were. It had been along time since they had last eaten and with all the aromas coming from the little shop their stomachs were starting to protest loudly.

The boys heard a sharp rapping sound and looked up. Inside the store there was a woman waving to them. "Oh no, I hope we're not in any trouble. My Uncle will get mad at us for sure." said Snuffles. They both opened the door and slowly headed inside.

"What are you two boys up to?" she asked. "Shouldn't you be in school?"

Realizing that they still had the head sets on and could understand everything that she said Snuffles replied, "Well miss, my Uncle Rufio is up talking with the King so we thought we would go to see the bay while we waited. Your bakery stopped us. It seems that we've forgotten to eat for a while and it smelled so good."

"Say, you aren't the boys that came from the outer world are you?" she interrupted.

"Yes, that's where we live." said Prickles all the time drooling over the meal worm and cinnamon breakfast rolls that were only about six inches from his face.

The shop owner smiled looking down at Prickles, "Well now we can't say that we starved our guests can we. Why don't you boys pick out a couple of rolls to eat. I can't have you dropping dead from starvation in my store now can I?" she asked looking straight into Prickles twinkling eyes.

Snuffles stopped Prickles in mid grab. "I'm sorry lady but we don't have any money to pay for them."

"Oh that's alright, from what I hear tell you boys are heros saving your little brother and helping to keep our world safe from the Loggerhedge. I guess I can afford to give our new heros breakfast. Now what do ya say," looking at Prickles, "which ones will it be?" Both boys grabbed two of the largest rolls that were in the case and thanked the lady while both cheeks were full. She laughed the whole time watching them eat the rolls and she waved goodbye as they left.

The further that Snuffles and Prickles traveled down the road toward the harbor the more village people they met along the way. Everyone seemed genuinely interested in who they were. When they reached the wharf area there were many tall sailing ships moored in the harbor. Snuffles wondered at how they could have gotten them into the harbor knowing they were so far under the ocean. As if reading their minds a tall sailor came up behind the and said, "They're beauties aren't they? None like um in the world."

"They sure are sir, but how did they get here?" asked Snuffles.

"Oh, that's the easy part. I wait till they sink. Then they're mine." he said.

"So how do you get them in here?" asked Prickles.

"Well, you see those big blokes over there," he pointed to the sea monsters. It was the first time that Snuffles and Prickles had laid their eyes on the large creatures. They were magnificent, all shapes, sizes and colors of the rainbow. Both the boys nodded in agreement at the sailors request. "Well I made a deal with their keepers and we get them to bring them into the harbor. They're the only ones strong enough to do it. I salvage what I can and if I need parts that I can't find here I use the salvage money I earn from selling it topside to buy what I need to rebuild them. So here they are in all their glory a kind of sailing museum."

Snuffles thought about the wonderful site and then was troubled, "Sir, what do you do with them now that they're rebuilt?" he asked.

"Oh that, well the King in all his wisdom thought that possibly our world could benefit by having a fleet of ships. So we take them out on the open sea and try to help stop the pirating and violence on the oceans." he said

Prickles just had to know, "Just how do you get them to the oceans, I mean there's a lot of water between here and there?" he asked.

"You see that archway next to the tunnel over there," they both nodded, "the king has a way to activate it and we can pass through without feeling the effects of the ocean. When it comes time to return a type of archway will appear in the ocean and we sail right through it and are back here where we belong."

The boys were very impressed and the sailor offered to take them out on his favorite ship for a tour. Afterwards he sailed them around the bay. Being on the water had such a relaxing effect on the boys that they thought they could fall asleep. A noise from the shore stopped their day dreaming and they focused on where the sound was coming from. Off in the distance they could make out two figures standing on the dock waving at them.

"Sir," Snuffles yelled up to the Sailor at the wheel house.

"What is it laddie?" he asked.

"Can you take us back to the dock now, I think that's my uncle over there waving at us?" Snuffles asked.

"We're on our way. Wouldn't want you in trouble with yer old man now, eh?" The sailor smiled as he looked at the boys. Both boys looked at him with grins on their faces and nodded in agreement.

"Well, it was short but boy did I have a lot of fun. What do you think happened at their meeting with the King?" Prickles asked.

"I don't know but I expect we're going to find out real soon. If they keep my Uncle I know that he is going to be very happy. I'm going to really miss him. He has been there for me all my life and not to have him around would be terrible and sad all at the same time."

As the ship came ashore the boys were greeted by Uncle Porcupine. He helped them to jump down from the ship and they thanked the sailor for the trip around the bay.

"Good ship lads," he said, "took to the sea with no problem at all. You come back and see me when you're ready to go again." and with that he waved at them and then turned back to stow the gear on the ship.

"Did you have fun," asked Rufio.

"We sure did, I never realized just how many creatures there are in this bay. The sailor took us right up next to most of them. Prickles even reached over and petted a couple of them." Said Snuffles. "How was your meeting with the King and when will we be able to see Hermie?" he asked.

"Well the King has told me that Hermie will need three days before he can come out of the infirmary. It will take that long to heal his burns. So we have that much time to explore all that we can together here in the village. After that the King has informed me that I must stay here. When you found the box in the cave that was the start of the chain of events that was supposed to happen and as it turns out this is to be my new home." Rufio explained to the boys.

"No!" yelled Snuffles, "It can't be. I found that box not you, it couldn't have anything to do with you. It's all my fault. What will I ever do without you in my life."

"Snuffles it's ok." Said Rufio as he reached for his nephew and pulled him in close and held him. They both were quiet for a few moment and just held onto each other. Snuffles was quietly sobbing while Rufio found it extremely hard to talk because of the lump in his throat.

"Think of it this way," Rufio said finally finding his voice again, "I will always be with you and you can know in your heart I didn't die."

"But you'll be gone and I won't get to see you ever again." He squeezed him tighter as he talked.

"All things are possible, Snuffles. Someday you may be looking out at the sea, or maybe just daydreaming in your secret cave and I'll try to find a way to come to you. You just wait and see." Rufio comforted Snuffle and Prickles a while longer and said, "Now I've heard from the bakery up the street that you both have had a very sugary breakfast but is there any room left for lunch."

Prickles with his bottomless pit for a stomach piped up, "Yep, I can always find room in here for a few more pieces of food." he said as he patted his round belly.

Snuffles still feeling a bit lost shrugged his shoulders and agreed that food was starting to sound pretty good to him too.

"Great and then after we have some lunch why don't we all head up to see Hermie. I'll bet he's getting pretty bored in the infirmary and could use some cheering up about now, OK?" asked Rufio. They all nodded in agreement.

Lunch went very well. Captain Heron took Snuffles, his uncle and Prickles back up the road to a small café that was dug halfway into an old cave. The people who owned it had made the front of the café to look like an old mine shaft and then appropriately named their café "The Shaft". Inside the café they continued the look by making it resemble a miners cabin. The tables had red and white checkered tablecloths but all the dishes were tin and there were old lanterns on each of the tables to light up the area. The seating was unique in that they were made of old logs and timbers cut in half. The walls of the café were covered with unusual miners gear. Head lamps, picks, ore buckets and other weird things a miner would use hung from the rafters and were stacked in the corners of the room. Miniature ore cars ran on a track throughout the café bringing the food from the kitchen out to the customers. The waitress came over to give them menu's and when Snuffles looked up at her he wanted to laugh. She had dirty old coveralls on and big mud boots. There were also heavy gloves in her belt. She would have looked very authentic with the exception that she had a hot pink bandana tied around her neck. She was wearing a miners hard hat with a lamp on it so she could find her way around the café. The waitress handed each of them a menu and when they opened it their mouths immediately started to water.

"I don't know whether I'm just really hungry or if its that everything sounds really good." said Uncle Porcupine.

"Well I don't know about sounding really good but everything in here smells great and I know I'm really hungry!" exclaimed Snuffles.

"Yea, what all he said and more." claimed an excited Prickles.

Captain Heron piped up, "I found this place by accident about a year ago and ever since I've been bringing all my friends here. The food is great and you get a lot to eat."

"That's good we wouldn't want these two boys to waste away to nothing now would we." Rufio laughed as he looked at the boys who now had mock anger on their faces.

Captain Heron was true to his words. The food was wonderful and just seemed to keep coming. At the end of dinner both Snuffles and Prickles leaned back in their chairs at the table rubbing their rather full and bulging bellies when Prickles said, "I think if I eat another bite I'll burst."

"I know what you mean, I think I might need to let my belt out a notch or two."

Both boys looked over at Uncle Porcupine and Captain Heron, they noticed that they also seemed a bit uncomfortable with all the food they had just eaten. Both men were leaning back as far as they could with their belly's extended, and were also moaning.

"Why did I eat that last plate of mealworm pate." groaned Rufio.

"I don't know about you but it was the grub buns that got me. I think I had about six too many." Captain Heron replied. They all looked at each other and broke into laughter. It was the first time that they had all truly felt relaxed in a long time.

About the time that everyone was considering curling up somewhere for a nap a bright light shone above their heads. They all looked up and the waitress was their to ask if anyone wanted dessert.

"Well now, you all are a sorry looking bunch. I just fed you and now that its time for dessert you all look like you're about to go to sleep. We have grub berry pie with June bug ice cream. Do I have any takers."

Both Snuffles and Prickles looked in each others eyes and then at the waitress and together they said, "We're in."

Rufio and Captain Heron moaned and pinched their fingers together indicating that they wanted very small pieces.

The waitress disappeared and brought back four of the largest bowls of pie and ice cream that you could ever imagine. The ice cream doubled the size of the bowl and was covered with chocolate, whip cream, nuts and cherries. Snuffle and Prickles looked at each other and grinned. "I'm already sick from being too full but, this is gonna be good." said Snuffles.

Everyone finished their deserts and then said good bye to the waitress. Back out in the streets they walked along the pathways heading up towards the castle. They were surprised at the way people would approach and speak with them. It was as if they had been part of the community all their lives. As long as the boys had the translation devices on they were able to speak freely with everyone without causing frustrations. Farther up the road they finally reached the junction that would take them to the local hospital. Snuffles was very anxious to see Hermie. He still felt a deep regret over his being there and especially about his getting hurt.

Rufio seemed to be reading his mind, "Snuffles, now don't you go getting your-self all worked up. There wasn't anything you could have done to prevent what happened to your brother. I think he would have gotten here all on his own somehow."

"How do you know that?" asked Snuffles.

"It just seems to me that whatever we've done seems to be part of some pre-designed plan. I've noticed that everything seems to be expecting us. I know that may sound silly but haven't you noticed the same things too?" Uncle Porcupine asked.

"You bet I have," answered Snuffles, "But I still feel really bad that Hermie got hurt."

"That's OK," replied Uncle Porcupine, "I do too, so let's go see him and find out when we will be able to take him home."

"OK, I brought him a bag of rolls from the dinner table I hope the nurses will let him have them." He said with a frown.

"Don't worry, I'm sure the nurses will let him have a few, I just hope they don't catch me with this bag of candy I brought him." Uncle Porcupine was holding up a bag of mixed candies must have weighed two pounds. Both looked at each other and started to laugh, a mischievous laugh of two boys trying to get away with something. So on they marched up to the hospital.

The group arrived at the top of the hill to a meadow filled with wild strawberries and tall grasses waving in the breeze.

Captain Heron said, "OK let's go in, but I gotta tell you the nurse on Hermie's floor is just about as sour a person as you would ever want to meet. I don't like her one bit and I know she doesn't like me."

Everyone looked at him in surprise. They had never know Captain Heron to express negative feeling about anyone before. Rufio gave the Captain a funny look and asked. "What did you do to make her mad at you Captain?"

The Captain shuffled his feet a bit and the looked Rufio straight in the eye, "I was visiting a friend in the hospital and brought him some treats. He didn't think he was being fed well enough. So, I thought a steak dinner was in order. I guess she could smell it because she practically chased me into his room. She took away the dinner and yelled at me telling me that if I ever tried to sneak in food again she'd kick me out but good. After that comment I left, but not before I told her she reminded me of an old hag I knew that lived in the gutter down by the wharf."

The others continued to stare at the Captain not believing what they were hearing. All Snuffles could think of was poor Hermie he never liked being around mean people and now it seemed that he was stuck with one for sure.

Snuffles and Uncle Porcupine looked at each other and then down at their bags full of the candy and rolls that they brought for Hermie. "What do you think, should we chance it or get rid of them now?" Snuffles asked.

"You only live once," replied Rufio, "What's the worst that can happen? She'll make us throw them out and yell. I'm willing to take a chance so that Hermie might get a little candy. Let's go." But then he stopped and looked around a little confused. He was standing in the middle of a field of strawberries. "Uh um, Captain Heron maybe you could explain what I'm doing in a field when we are supposed to be going to the hospital to see my nephew?"

The Captain broke out with a big laugh. He had been waiting for just this very moment. He wasn't sure just how long it would take for them to realize where they were. "Well now Rufio, don't go getting yourself all in an uproar. You should know by now that in this world things are not always as they seem." Captain Heron then walked over to a gong that was on the edge of the field and rang it three times with a small mallet that was attached by a rope. The breeze that had been blowing started to gust even harder until Snuffles and Prickles thought that they would be blown over. The air in front of them over the field started to shimmer and a modern four story building appeared. "Wow that was great," both Snuffles and Prickles chimed in together. In front of them now stood a mirrored glass building that reflected the surrounding field in such a way that the hospital looked like a field of strawberries. The area was so well disguised that you almost didn't need the invisibility machine.

"Many years ago when we had terrible wars the hospital was always under attack. We housed a lot of the prisoners and wounded here so naturally this became a high security risk area. The King and his advisors felt that we could better protect those injured by the installation of a invisibility machine and so far it has worked." explained the Captain.

"Yes, but this is a hospital, everyone who gets sick would eventually know where it is." said Rufio.

"That's true, but for a few select people and the guard everyone who visits or is a patient here is given a drug to make them forget and so far it's worked." Everyone went quiet looking at the door they were about to enter.

"Are they going to make us forget everything?" asked Prickles.

"Oh no," said Captain Heron, "as a matter of fact, they are not going to make you forget anything. You see I have friends in high places. When you go home, that's when they will erase your memories of the hospital. OK?"

The boys nodded and they proceeded up the stairs and through the doors to find Hermie.

The front entrance to the hospital was in the shape of the King's head and the doorway opened through his mouth.

"I feel like I'm going to be eaten," said Snuffles.

"I know what you mean. This is kind of weird. I hope he's not hungry!"

Uncle Porcupine and Captain Heron went up to the main desk and asked the nurse where Hermie's room was. She pointed to where the stairs were and Rufio motioned for the boys to follow him.

Chapter 16

Hermie's Hospital Room

All the hallways leading to Hermie's room were clean and white and gave you a feeling of being cold and sterile. At the end of each corridor sat a nurse. Snuffles felt as if he was under a microscope when they looked at both he and Prickles.

"I don't think they like us very much." Prickles whispered to Snuffles.

"I hear you there. I don't think I like them very much either."

A big round stern faced nurse stood up and peered over the top of her desk. "And just where do you think you're going?" she asked in a gruff tone to Uncle Porcupine.

"Oh," said Uncle Porcupine in a startled voice, "we were just about to go and see my nephew, Hermie. I believe he's in the room at the end of the hall on this floor."

She looked down at the boys, "Well you can go to see the boy but these children will have to stay out here. There's no telling what germs they're carrying."

Snuffles and Prickles started to protest loudly when Uncle Porcupine held up his hand to silence them. He then looked straight at the nurse, "You mean to tell me that you would deny this boy," he said pointing at Snuffles, "the right to see his brother. By whose orders do you follow?" He questioned.

Looking a bit out of sorts the nurse shuffled the papers on her desk and the looked up and straight into Rufio's eyes, "The King's if you must know."

Rufio's quills jumped straight up, "I think we should contact the King right now. I think that you're lying. King Jerod happens to be a friend of mine and I can't think of any possible reason he would deny access to my nephew. So if you don't have any better reason than that, step aside, Snuffles and I'll be seeing my nephew and his brother now!" With that being said Rufio marched around the nurse who had her hand on her hips trying to look very cross and headed down the hall to Hermie's room.

As the boys followed Snuffle's Uncle, Prickles turned around waved at her, and with a big grin on his face he reached into his pocket and grabbed a small handful of candy which he tossed at her. The candy flew in a hundred different directions on the floor. She waved her fisted hands at him and grunted loudly and hurried about cleaning up the mess.

"Maybe that will sweeten her up, you think?" he snickered to Snuffles as both boys were laughing at the sight.

"Let's hope so because I don't think she's going to be telling people nice things about us." replied Snuffles.

"Oh, I don't care." he laughed, "I've got you to help protect me." and he threw his arm around Snuffles shoulder.

They both giggled the rest of the way down the long hall until they came to Hermie's door. Uncle Porcupine knocked softly and slowly opened the door.

Inside the room it looked like a toy store instead of a hospital room and in the middle of the room sat Hermie. "What on earth is going on?" Uncle Porcupine exclaimed as he turned to look at Captain Heron, who had been especially quiet up until now.

Hermie was a sight. You could hardly tell him apart from all the stuffed animals in the room. Snuffles looked down at the bag of rolls he had brought for Hermie to eat and decided that there was no way he would be able to compare with the room full of gifts and candy that were already there. He decided to not say anything about it. Snuffles noticed that his Uncle must have had the same idea because he saw him putting his bag into his pocket as well.

Hermie looked as good as new. He had a rosy face and looked happy. "I sure have missed all you guys," he said as he jumped up to hug everyone. "Why did it take so long for you to come and see me?" he asked.

"They told us you couldn't have any visitors until now." replied Uncle Porcupine giving Captain Heron a suspicious look.

"Now look here Rufio," started the Captain, "all I know is that I was told to take you around the town and show you a good time. Honest that's all. And as for all this stuff, well, the town folk thought it was really neat to have a child visitor from the outer world and they wanted to make him feel welcome. I guess they got a little out of hand. But they meant well."

"Well, I guess that will be another question the King will have to answer for me as to why we have been kept from seeing Hermie," said Rufio holding his nephew on his lap.

"When will you get out of here?" Prickles asked Hermie.

"I don't know, they say I'm all better. I want to go with you now Uncle, can I?" whined Hermie.

Before Rufio could answer Captain Heron spoke, "You'll have to be patient a little while longer. I have to take your Uncle to see the King. As a matter of fact we should be going to the castle now."

"Wow, I've been wanting to get a look at the castle let's go" piped Snuffles.

"I'm sorry, Snuffles but the King has requested that you and Prickles stay here with your brother. This is kind of a formal meeting with some of the advisors and your Uncle. They need to discuss his new life in the inner world along with yours and how you'll be going home."

Snuffles and Prickles were both on their feet ready to protest when Uncle Porcupine spoke, "Now I know what you're going to say, but we talked about this already. You know that certain things have to be worked out so I can get the three of you back home and at the rate it's going there's going to be a lot of explaining involved as it is. Let's just wait and see what the King has in store for us. You and Prickles sit tight here with Hermie and I'll be back before you know it. Hopefully with answers this time."he gave them all a big hug and turned to Captain Heron and said, "Well, we had better not keep the King waiting for long." As the two men left the room everyone stared quietly at the closing door.

"I wonder if I'll ever get to see him again." Snuffles said out loud.

"I sure hope so, I really like him a lot."said Prickles.

Hermie picked up an armful of stuffed toys and silently sat down in a corner with them to wait.

Chapter 17

The Castle

W hen Rufio and the captain arrived back at the castle he was amazed at just how large it was inside. The corridors were long and dark and the floor was lined with diamond shaped stones. There was a smell of dampness in the air which chilled you to the bone if you were standing for long periods of time on the stone floors. Guards and doormen were posted at every turn, "I'll bet even the King has trouble finding his way through this maze of corridors let alone feeding all these people." said Rufio with a hushed voice. Captain Heron just laughed and lead Rufio down corridors that seemed to never end. After fifteen minutes or so they came upon a pair of giant double doors. Captain Heron pulled up short, "I'm sorry Rufio, but I'm going to have to ask you to wait out here while I go in for a few moments to see if they're ready for you."

"That's OK, I understand," replied Rufio. Down deep inside his emotions were getting the better of him. He tried to calm himself down as Captain Heron disappeared through the doors into the chamber beyond. Once gone Rufio's imagination began to run wild. It was the first chance he'd had to look around and see just how unusual the corridors were decorated. The pictures on the walls were of what Rufio guessed, different battles, and the prizes in each of the pictures glowed with an eerie luminescence. This made the pictures somewhat life like in appearance. The people in them seemed to turn and watch you as you moved about the room. Rufio didn't know what substance caused the glowing but he made a special note in his mind to find out what it was.

About the time that Rufio was going to turn down one last corridor Captain Heron appeared from the Kings chambers. "Rufio, over here." he waved. "They're ready for you now."

Rufio gave a start at his name being called, "Uh, ok. Let's go." He took a deep breath and followed the Captain Heron into the chamber.

Chapter 18

The King Jerod's Chamber

When Rufio entered the chambers he was surprised at the enormous size of the room. Light seemed to be illuminating from every corner by what looked like oblong shaped glowing disks. Rufio was curious about the disk and what they were made of. When they had finished their talk with the King he hoped he might be able to examine them more closely. He followed the Captain along the carpeted strip that ran down the center of the room all the way to where he could see King Jerod sitting in the middle of a u-shaped table smiling and waiting for him.

The King had six other people sitting with him. Rufio learned that to the right of the King sat the Administer of Transportation, the Administer of Foreign Elements and Magic, the Administer of Relations and on the Kings left sat the Administer for Non-Interference and Contamination Between Worlds, the Administer for Protection and Rights, and the Administer of Advice. During their conversation, Rufio soon realized that these men had a great deal of advice to offer the King and he seemed to considered their words greatly.

As Rufio stood there for quite some time, the King never looked in his direction, he wondered if he had seen him enter at all. He was about to address him when he looked up from his conversation and smiled. "Oh, Rufio my dear friend. The time has come to work out the details of your life among us here in Atlantahedge. As you know, by now, our world has many secrets and we must be especially careful to protect our citizens in Atlantahedge. We must guard those secrets with our very lives. That brings us to the matter about your nephews and their friend. Usually when we except outsiders into our world we don't have many problems. Their entrance to our world has been foretold many months before they arrive. Either they are older, such as yourself, or something tragic has happened to them so as not to make their disappearance noticed. But, in the case of your nephews we seem to have a whole new dilemma happening. Not only is he and his friend a youngling but they most certainly will be missed. We have been discussing different ways in which to get them back to their families and still protect the citizens from exposure here to the outer world at the same time. Our prime minister of foreign elements and magic has researched his books on this situation and has come up with a solution for all of us. We will be sending the boys back in time to almost the exact moment in which they opened the box at your home. The difference this time is that the lock on the box will not be open nor will it be able to. They will search for you and you will be nowhere to be found. They will return home to tell their mother you are missing. Do you have any questions?"

Rufio thought about what the King had said and, "But King Jerod? The boys know just about everything that goes on here, they'll still remember it if they go back to their own time, they'll tell everyone about their adventures."

"I've thought that through," said King Jerod, "We have a special draft that we give to people when they have stumbled onto our world in the past, we'll give it to the boys just as they are about to be transported back to their world. It will make short term memory a blur and what they do remember they will think is a dream."

"I don't think I want my nephew to forget me!" I exclaimed.

"Rufio," the King said softly, "it has to be done for the safety of our world."

Rufio nodded in agreement but was saddened by the thought that the adventures he and his nephews shared would be lost forever and that he would be nothing more than a memory to the boys. "When will this be taking place?" Rufio asked the King.

"Just as soon as we are through here. We'll take you back to the infirmary and let you have the rest of the day to say goodbye. Then tonight at the approximate time the boys opened the box originally we'll send the boys back home."

"Alright." Said Rufio reluctantly.

The King stood up and walked around the table to where Rufio stood with his head down lost in thought. He put his arm around Rufio and started to walk him away from the advisors still sitting at the table. "Rufio," the King said quietly, "I don't want your time here to be sad. When the boys go back the box will disappear and materialize back at the cave where the boys first found it. Your nephew will be called back to it in a few months after the shock of your disappearance has passed. He will find it and open the box and from that point on he will find he has an open portal to you. You will have your own alarm that when the box is opened you can see Snuffles and have short conversations with him. By that time we will be able to teach you about what you can and cannot say about our world here. I hope that will help you in your endeavors to continue to be a part of his life as he grows up. I wish it could be more."

"Are you kidding," Rufio smiled, "All I wanted was to keep in touch and help him with things when he needs advice that his mother couldn't give him. Now I'll be able to do just that. You couldn't have made me happier. Thank you so much."

Rufio excused myself from the King's chambers and hurried back to the boys at the hospital. Along the way everything seemed to be brighter and lighter. He felt that the he and the boys would have a wonderful afternoon after all. As he hurried down the hospitals corridor toward the room where the boys were Rufio couldn't help but feel that everything would work out.

Chapter 19

The Journey Home

*A*s Rufio entered the room where the boys were staying he couldn't help but notice that the boys had chosen one corner and were sitting quietly with each other. "What's all this sad and gloomy look about this place?" He asked.

Snuffles face started to beam with a grand smile and he rushed to his uncle's waiting arms. "I'm so glad you're back. I've been worried. What did the King say? How long before we can all go home? Can we get out of here sometime soon?"

"Hold on Snuffles," Rufio hushed, "take a breath for a minute. King Jerod and I discussed a lot of the details about what is going to happen later tonight and I think I need to make sure that everyone understands what is going to happen."

"Tonight! That soon! Great we'll be home with Mama. I can't wait. Tomorrow we can check all the things that have happened around the town." Prickles said excitedly.

"Well, there is a few problems with that theory Prickles and I'm afraid there won't be as many changes as you would hope for." said a somber Rufio.

"Tell us what's going to happen Uncle," asked Snuffles?

"The King and his advisors have thought through all the repercussions of our visits in their world and have come to some decisions on how we are to return the three of you to your world. You see when we left the kitchen in my house certain events would be put in motion. For instance, your disappearing for this long and then reappearing suddenly would spark a lot of questions. How would you be able to answer and still keep this world protected?" Rufio asked.

"I don't know, but couldn't I just say we ran away." answered Snuffles.

"You could try that for a while but somewhere down the line you might tell someone in secret or just slip up under the pressure of being constantly asked the same questions over and over again." said Rufio.

"I would not! I can keep a secret." said Snuffles.

"I know that you can but, what about your brother. Hermie is very young. Are you willing to stake the lives and the secrecy of these people on an accident." asked Rufio.

"So how are we getting home Uncle?" came a small voice from the corner. Rufio had almost forgotten where Hermie was. Sitting in the corner like that he looked like one of the stuffed animal toys piled up in it.

"Well my little Hermie, don't you worry, you and your brother will be going home tonight. Unfortunately I won't be joining you. As you know the King had thought that maybe it was a mistake about the box being opened so soon. But, that was not the case. The series of events prior to it being opened all happened as it should and my time in the outer world is done."

"Uncle that can't be right. I found the treasure chest and brought it to you. If it was a key to you leaving then why was it left buried in an old cave?" cried Snuffles.

"That's just the point. The box would get to me however possible when the time came. It just used you and Prickles as the messengers. Don't be sad. Since I've been here I have felt more alive than I have felt in years. I'll be able to keep on having adven-tures and I'll keep on living a useful and productive life. Most importantly the King has promised me I'll be able to look in on you and your brothers and sisters from time to time." Rufio said.

"I don't know how I can keep on going if I don't have you around Uncle. I'll miss you too much." Rufio held Snuffles and Hermie until they found control of their emotions. Snuffles then said quietly. "I guess it will be OK if I get to see you once in a while and you can tell me all about what you are doing. I also have the memories of what we did together here and that's good."

"I'm sorry but that's something else I have to tell you. Tonight when they get ready to send you home they are going to give you a draft that will change your memories of what has happened to you here. When you get back to my kitchen you will find the box locked and unopenable. After you go back to your homes the box will disappear. I'm sorry I can't make it any easier but I now know this is for the best." The boys were on their feet instantly arguing with Rufio, "Forget! We won't forget. That's not fair. I don't want to forget. We can't forget you Uncle!"

"I'm sorry that's the way it has to be. No exceptions. I wish I could do more but you just need to trust me on this. I too, will be missing you."

Rufio tried to quiet them down and after a while offered to take them out with the time they had left for ice cream. They protested a bit more but reluctantly agreed to go.

Later that evening when Rufio and the boys returned to the hospital and were met by King Jerod and his advisors. They smiled at the boys and the King tried to reassure them of what was about to happen.

"I want each of you to know that if I knew of any other way to get you home and still protect my world I would. But, at this time, this is the best plan."

"Just what are you going to do to us?" asked Snuffles.

"Well you will be taking a trip back in time. We don't normally allow this type of trip except only on rare occasions. When we give the potion for time travel it causes a molecular change in the body.

Then we can transport you through our time and into another time. We have to be carful not to give to much or to little of the portion so as not to over shoot or under shoot the time that we want the person to be left in. The reason for putting you into a deep sleep is so that when you go through the molecular change you won't feel any discomfort as it is happening. Do you have any questions?" said the King.

"Why can't my uncle come with me?" said the littlest voice.

The King looked down at Hermie and said, "The reason that you were able to unlock the box so easily, my dear friend, was because you uncle's time in your world is over. I don't know what was going to happen to him, whether he was going to be hurt, or sick or killed in some way, but the box was told to know when it was going to happen and help him leave before he was in any pain. That's why he must stay here. If we return him, with you back to your world he will surely die. Knowing that your uncle will be safe with us here is better than waiting for him to die, don't you think?"

"I guess so, but I'm going to miss him a lot." Hermie started to sniffle and Rufio reached out and put his arm around him.

"You know somewhere or somehow I'll find a way to check in on you from time to time and see how you're holding up. So you better be a good boy and help your brothers and sisters and especially your mom, got it?" said Rufio.

"Got it." said Hermie and he hugged Rufio harder knowing that when he let go it would probably be the for the last time.

The Kings Advisor, Aerostatis, the administer of foreign elements and magic walked forward towards the boys and said, "Now is the time for you young gentlemen to each climb up on the beds and the nurse will insert a tube into your arm so that we can use it to put the potion in." The boys obeyed feeling a bit robotic and were soon hooked up to the monitors.

"We use the monitors to make sure that your body is accepting the potion," Aerostatis said.

Rufio walked up to each of the boys and hugged them one last long goodbye. His eyes were so full of tears that he choked on his words when he tried to speak. After a minute he decided to just step back and let fate happen.

Aerostatis then instructed the nurse to inject his potion into the tubes while he explained, "All this potion does is make you very sleepy. Until we are able to detect that you are in a deep sleep, we can't go any further. Don't try to fight it or it will just take a lot longer to work."

Rufio picked up the boys hands and quietly said to them, "Look at me boys, look deep into my eyes, I want to be your last sight here and I want you to know that nothing bad is going to happen to you. I will make sure of that. I will always be with you in your hearts." They all stared into each others eyes for what seemed an eternity. This seemed to calm the boys down and they were soon in a deep sleep. Rufio looked up at Aerostatis and said, "What happens now?"

"Now we'll take them down to the wharf and put them into the transporter. I didn't want to take them there before they fell asleep and alarm them about what was going to be happening next."

The nurses brought in three gurneys and the boys were lifted onto them. Rufio stared intently at each of the boys faces to memorize every feature, then they wheeled them out of the room and loaded them onto the cart to go to the wharf.

Chapter 20

What's Next?

The warehouse was dark when they pulled up in front and there seemed to be no life about the place. King Jerod pushed a button mounted to the top of the cart and a large rolling door slid up very fast and quietly. They proceeded to drive inside and down numerous corridors until they came into a large room with a lot of electronic equipment. Rufio was surprised. He hadn't seen evidence of any real technology before now. King Jerod was standing looking at Rufio and laughed. "Don't be so surprised. We do know what a computer and keyboard are, we just choose the older, more simpler ways as the best way to live out our lives here."

"Wow, you really fooled me. I would have never guessed that this type of stuff existed in this world.," commented Rufio.

"Over here." yelled out one of the technicians. "We need to get started soon. We've calibrated the instruments to today's time and need get the boys into the chambers while the machines are ready to go.

Everyone moved into high speed and the three gurneys were pushed to the door of the transporter. Rufio and Captain Heron carefully picked each one of the boys up and placed them onto the floor. Rufio took a moment to kiss each one goodbye and secretly slipped a note into the front pocket of Snuffles pants. As he came out of the door of the transporter he motioned to the technician that all was ready inside. Aerostatis then walked over to the control panel and handed instructions to the technician who then proceeded to enter the coordinates into the computer. With everyone watching intently the chamber began to glow brightly and soon became a blinding white light so intense that even with your hand over your eyes you still had to turn away.

Within seconds the light stopped and Rufio hurried up to the window to look into the chamber and they were gone.

"Do you know where they are?" Rufio asked Aerostatis with shock on his face.

"We can actually show what is going on while the system is still attached to the boys aura's." Aerostatis led Rufio over to a different monitor and preceded to punch in the boys coordinates and after a few minutes of static a picture started to form. The boys were sitting in front of the television watching a movie planning what they were going to do about the chest they found and how soon they could get back to their Uncle's burrow and retrieve the chest. "This is the part where we can alter history a little bit to help out their lives." Said Aerostatis and with the flip of a switch the boy's aura's were superimposed into the time warp right over the boys on the screen. "Now we'll be able to see how the story changes in the days ahead to catch up to our time now."

Rufio sat and watched intently as the story unfolded in front of his eyes.

Snuffles started to speak, "I think if we're lucky, we should be able to get to my uncle's burrow and sneak in the back of the kitchen without being noticed. Then we can take it out behind the old barn and open it. If all goes well, we would be back here and in bed before anyone knows we're gone."

"That sounds like a good plan I just hope we can pull it off." Said Prickles.

The boys planned the details on how they would sneak out of the burrow after everyone had gone to bed. While waiting, night seemed to go on forever, when finally Snuffles' mom came in to tuck them into bed and say goodnight.

Both boys waited for as long as they could but the drug that was still in their system took effect and Snuffles and Prickles were asleep in no time at all.

"Now that we have changed that part of their lives lets keep watching to see if the out come is what we need." said Aerostatis.

In the morning the boys awoke abruptly and were shocked to find themselves in bed. "Boy we really messed things up by falling asleep last night." said Prickles.

"I guess we were really tired. Oh well, let's get dressed and get over to Uncle Porcupines burrow and see if he got any answers for us." Snuffles said.

They quickly dressed and ran downstairs. Mom had made breakfast but the boys each grabbed a muffin, waved goodbye and ran out the door. On the way to Uncle Porcupine's burrow they talked about how rich they were going to be and what they would do with the money when they opened the chest. About the time they were dreaming of owning a race car they reached the back door of Snuffle's Uncle's burrow. Snuffles knocked loudly on the back door.

"That's strange, he should have answered the door by now." Snuffles commented.

Prickles was standing on his tip toes looking in the window and said, "You know the lights on in the kitchen and there's a lot of things on the table as well."

"I wonder where he could be." Snuffles said with a look of curiosity on his face.

Prickles wiggled the door handle. "Hey Snuffles the back doors open. Want to go in?"

"Sure, maybe my Uncle is just asleep and he forgot to lock up last night."

They opened the door and walked into the kitchen. It seemed very quiet almost too quiet but they didn't let it stop them. They checked over the whole house and found nothing. The one thing that was missing besides Uncle Porcupine was the chest.

"Where do you think it is?" asked Prickles.

"I don't know but wherever it is I'll bet it's with my Uncle."

They searched for both the chest and Rufio for the better part of two hours and never found a trace of either one. Finally they decided to go and tell Snuffles' mom about what had been going on up to that point and see if she had any advice.

"Where is the chest I thought you said it would be there." Rufio questioned.

"It was last night. It disappeared to its new location by now. The boys didn't go to your burrow last night and after a certain time it moved on." said Aerostatis.

When the boys got home Snuffles' mom listened very intently to what they had to say. "Well Snuffles that was sure an interesting find for the two of you. I think I'll go over to your Uncles burrow and see what I can find out for myself." Mom then grabbed her jacket and headed for the door. The boys went along out of curiosity.

Once back at Rufio's burrow Snuffles mom went inside and looked high and low for Rufio and the chest but she also came up empty handed.

"I think we are going to just let things be for a couple of days and see if your Uncle has just gone off on one of his wild trips. If he's not back in two days we'll get the inspectors out here to look over the situation." Said Snuffles Mom. The boys agreed and Snuffles Mom locked up Rufio's burrow and everyone left to go home.

After two days of waiting and still no Uncle, Snuffles mom decided to notify the inspectors and turn in a missing persons report on her brother. She had sent Snuffles up to clean his room to keep him out of her way as she phoned the inspectors. Snuffles went upstairs grumbling about having to work when it would be a lot more interesting to sit and listen.

Snuffles was just about done cleaning his room when his mom called up to let him know that she was on her way to meet the inspectors at his Uncles burrow and that if he would like to go along he should grab a jacket and come down. Snuffles looked around his room that was starting to get that clean lived in look and spotted his favorite vest stuffed in a corner. "Ah ha, that's the one I want," he said. Snuffles picked it up and threw it on. He looked quickly in the mirror and brushed back his quills and turned towards the door. As he turned he shoved both his hand into his pockets and stopped in his tracks. Inside he felt a piece of paper that he knew wasn't there before. He pulled the paper out of his pocket, opened it and read out loud, "Please remember me. I will love you always and I will find a way to watch over you. One day you will find me if you remember. Tell no one about this letter. I am trusting you with my life. Love Rufio." As Snuffles read the letter his face turned pale but he knew he would do what his Uncle asked of him and he knew he would always remember him.

At Uncle Porcupines burrow the inspectors went through everything inside and found no clues as to the whereabouts of Uncle Porcupine. Snuffles watched as they searched the property for him knowing very well they were not going to find him. After several hours they exhausted their efforts and called a halt to the search. They told Snuffles' Mom, who was now quite distraught over the matter, that they would keep in touch. Snuffles hugged his mom as they closed up the burrow and headed home.

Many months have gone by and the search for Uncle Porcupine was called off. He was listed as missing. Mom thinks someone took him and he was possible killed. I don't think that could have happened because there was never a ransom note. She's very sad and thinks we should have a funeral for him. So, next week we're having a funeral for Uncle Porcupine. The town put up a memorial for him because of his military service and his work in the community. On the other hand, I don't know what to think about a funeral that has no one being buried. I think it's a little weird.

I look at the letter that Uncle Porcupine left me every day and I can't help but think that I will see him very soon. I just wish he had told me where and how. Prickles and I go to the cave as much as we can. We both feel more free there than at home these days. We never found our treasure chest again and all I think of is that wherever Uncle Porcupine is that's where our treasure chest is. Well I'll put Uncle Porcupine's note away in my hiding box and get to the cave. Prickles just called and said he found something buried in the walls and needs my help to get it out.

9 781456 844837